Number 47

Hannah R. Palmer

Acknowledgements

Thanks to Nicola, my Mum, Jackie and Gary for reading and critiquing Number 47 early on and giving me some much needed steer. Thank you Dan for telling me that I could do it and being the creative voice of reason that I've grown so used to. And thanks to Sean Stone, who has quite literally given me too many pointers throughout this process to list off.

And finally, thank you to anyone reading this novel. Even if just one person enjoys this book, then I'll consider it a success.

My knees are wet. Cold water is lifting from the sodden earth, penetrating the denim of my hand-me-down jeans, climbing up my thighs. The dark blue fabric becomes stiff and abrasive; coarse against my small, knobbly knees. "Footballers knees", a familiar voice from way back reminds me. The water is seeping, bleeding into my flesh, coursing along my shins. The droplets are there, floating and weaving between the woven fabric of my trousers. They find a new place to take a breather, a new place to crawl between and hide. I bet they feel safe.

The weight of my body pushes into the soil beneath my legs, cradling my calves in the soft clay. It's making a mould of me, a way to remember the shape of my body, a way to preserve my memory.

I'm kneeling on his grave. My body hovering above his, my hands feet away from him, separated only by earth. He's resting down there, his hands crossed on his chest like a mummy. He's so peaceful, I think - so calm and so still. And I'm still here, still stuck above ground paying for this - whatever this is. I lay my trembling palm on the headstone to remind myself of the permanence of his absence, to remind myself that there's no coming back - there's no waking up. The cold, wet marble shocks my palm, awakens my fingertips.

I trace over his name, running my finger through the deep grooves in the headstone, sliding dark green, algae-like grime away from the grey marble and onto my fingertip. I spell his name. I say it out loud to remind   myself. *He was such a gentle boy, such a loving boy. I feel so much older than my years.*

A voice cracks the silence above my head.

'Time to go', it says. Emotionless, very matter-of-fact. The voice's hand is on my shoulder, pressing into old bruises, pulling me up off the floor.
I wince and obey, rising slowly and smudging mud from my knees, smearing it across the light denim. I don't question the voice's command anymore.
'Goodbye, Noah,' I whisper.

Chapter One

I'm staring again. Gazing at the back of his head, eyes drifting down to the nape of his neck, just above the collar of his shirt as he hovers in the queue. My eyes slip like a droplet of water gliding over the dips and troughs of his clear, olive skin. He's beautiful. I can't allow it to sink in—how perfect he is. I could list all of the perfections this man possesses, all of the many powers he has up his pristinely pressed shirtsleeves. But let's be honest, that would be boring. I've sat here and had days, weeks, maybe even a month's worth of hours to meticulously study this creature - every inch of his skin, every crease in his face, his hands, his eyes. Maybe I'm not willing to share that much of him just yet.

He pays the barista with a warm smile. Two gentle creases form at the corner of his mouth as he drops the loose change into a mug marked 'tips' by the till. He waits, makes small talk with the staff. He's slipped his hands into his back pockets the way I like, standing relaxed but strong. He's in control; I feel protected by him. I worry that if I look away, I'll realise he's really a figure of my imagination and he'll disappear altogether. If I break eye contact with him, he'll realise I'm a fraud and he couldn't possibly be in love with someone like me. And without him, I'm nothing. I know a lot of people say that sort of thing and generally speaking I'm not an old romantic, but it's how I feel. It's how he makes me feel. He gives me a purpose–gives me a reason to get up in the morning and come here at 11 a.m. on the dot for a latte and a read of the tabloids. To make him smile is the purpose of my day and not being in love with him would destroy me. Our veins are intertwined, our arteries plaited, our lives hooked together in a way I simply can't explain.

The barista thuds the metal jug on the worktop, the milk jumping and turning over on itself until smooth white glossy waves of cream rest on the surface. Her arms flex as she bangs out the air holes, crashing the metal container against the faux-marble counter with a thud. Details are what make the scene; details are what I remember most. I watch as he walks the fresh coffee over to the table, nestling my own in front of me as I wait, letting the heat radiate through my palms. Speaking would spoil the moment, so I leave the room to be quiet, bar the hustle and bustle of shoppers and other workers on their breaks. The aroma of the coffee is soothing and aromatic. I'm happy - he's happy. We only have twenty minutes or so together before we return to work, but that's plenty of time to just be thankful for each other's company and I'm blissfully ignorant of the passing of time.

The daily crossword has lost my attention. I'd given up a while ago anyway, given up on the clues and the hints and started jamming any old word that would fit into the grey boxes. My attention span is short, unless it concerns him - he has my attention 100%, any time of the day. I watch him, study him, memorise every little thing there is to know about him. Two lumps of brown sugar in his coffee, three stirs clockwise with the teaspoon which is placed delicately on the saucer once used, leaving the tiniest bit of pale brown liquid cradled amongst the polished steel. He grabs the mug by the smooth white body of the cup—never through the handle.

It's the little things, the reassurance of routine that reminds me over and over again just how truly lucky I am—how perfect being in love is. How sickeningly happy I feel. How jealous my mother would be of my own happiness. How much I want to brag about it to her, to rub it in her face, to hold her head down in my happiness until she drowns. I sip my coffee and the warmth of the sweet liquid bolsters my euphoria. I can't imagine life any other way.

The minute hand of the old clock behind the till slips further down, falling closer to the floor. He licks a fleck of white foam from his top lip, a flash of pink tongue against his rough-shaven face. He has a meeting this afternoon, I can tell. He only ever carries his briefcase here if he needs to dash to a meeting straight after our daily coffee. And just like that, as the clock behind the till reads 11:30, he slides the empty mug away, stands up and leaves. He's so predictable. I follow until we reach the door, holding it open for him as we go our separate ways.

'Goodbye,' I mouth the words after him and watch for a few seconds as he walks away.

He works for a local banking firm—has done since we met in school. Worked his way up from intern to some fancy title or other that I can't quite remember. He does well for himself, I know that much. I work for a charity a few minutes down the road and do slightly less well for myself, but I'm not bitter about that. I'm happy where I am; close enough to smell his cologne in the air but without treading on each other's toes. I value our space. The café is the perfect spot for us to meet during our breaks. We work so closely together that I can see into his office from my desk. I can see him work, see him eat his lunch alone, and see the exact moment that he leaves. I never have to take my eyes off him.

A quick glance at my watch breaks me out of my usual daydream. I've been standing in the same spot watching him walk away for minutes without even realising it. He consumes me. I swing my satchel back over my shoulder and work my way through the bustling streets to my own office.

The warm, midday sun presses against my window, heating the office to an unbearable clammy temperature. Sweat rests on my top lip, the occasional bead slipping over the edge and spreading its salty taste on my tongue. The white light from my computer screen adds to the stifling heat, its low, droning hum buzzing around the room. I can't concentrate–I rarely can. I click my pen on and off a few times, type a few lines into an email with the sole purpose of deleting them seconds later–anything to appear busy enough to warrant my paycheque. The humming seems to be getting louder, the drone upgrading itself to a steady crackle of white noise that fills my ears like cotton wool. It gets louder until there's nothing else I can focus on. It crescendos and intensifies and makes me feel hopelessly dizzy. I look down to see the notes I was taking smeared across the page in a sweaty smudge, the remnants of the words transferred onto the heel of my palm. The noise fills my head–the incessant buzzing of the wasp tapping and crashing against my skull, scratching and itching behind my eyes.

'Meet him again, Sarah?'

I swing around in my chair. I know who's speaking without looking; there's no mistaking that nasally voice. Ellis is full of herself, but I know how important it is to play her game, to go through the motions. She's quite a poisonous character, whether intentionally or not. It doesn't bother me, actually. I quite like it. I'm happy someone is showing interest in me and I'm even happier that she's too dim to realise how much I take advantage of her. I want her to know about him, to spread how happy I am. I want to show him off and parade him around the office. It's flattering, her showing such an interest in me. I love the idea of making her jealous so I play up to it.

'Maybe,' I say, with a coquettish grin. She's envious, I know it, but frankly, I enjoy it. I love having power over her. She's always so smug and yet I'm the one sat here toying with her, dangling my perfect relationship in her face and teasing her with it. I can see she's desperate for more and who am I to deny her that privilege? She thinks she's the one with the power, but really I'm the one manipulating her. I want her to know, I want her to watch me from the other side of the office. I want her to want me.

'He was wearing the most perfect, crisp white polo shirt today. Looked like some kind of model, no word of a lie. I'm really lucky to have him.'

I over-enunciate my words, flicking them between my teeth like a dog with a cheap chew toy, my eyes never leaving hers. I could do this to her all day. It's so easy to make her radiate green I've become almost addicted to it. Seeing the pang of envy dart across her eyes gives me an unmistakable hit of endorphins. She's pathetic and I relish it. I hover the heel of my stiletto over her pathetic throat, threatening to push my weight down and drive the spike deeper and deeper.

'Well, glad to hear you're happy.' Her words could not sound less sincere. She throws a forced smile across her face and walks off back to her end of the corridor. Honestly, it's like she doesn't know how to be happy for anyone else. I almost feel sorry for her, in a way, sashaying back to her tiny desk in her tiny tight skirt in search of more information to amuse her for the day. How small minded and unhappy she must be on the inside.

The rest of the afternoon is horribly uneventful. All I can focus on is the promise of walking home with him. Bumping into him outside the coffee shop and taking the short walk to our separate homes to spend the night. Maybe tonight will be the night he asks me inside to stay. Maybe it won't be. I'm not going to set my heart on it. Everything is going so well, so according to plan that I wouldn't dare ask in case I made the situation awkward. In case he wasn't ready or thought I was moving too fast. No, I'll let him make that move. I shuffle some papers across my desk, file a few things and fire off a handful of important looking emails to various benefactors. I consider teasing Ellis some more and figure she can wait until tomorrow. I'll be seeing him again then anyway.

My eyes start drifting around four o'clock, sliding away from the computer screen and up to the corner of the ceiling. The noises of the office get louder, the words of each email blurrier. I've lost all interest in my job for this afternoon. There's nowhere less inspiring than an office block. My mind wanders out of the window, down a few floors and through the open blinds of the building next door. His offices back onto mine in a coincidence that was effectively written in the stars. He's just walking in. I watch as he barrels through the door and dumps his briefcase on the floor. He throws himself into the nearest leather armchair, swinging his feet up onto the desk in front of him. He's small and slightly obscured from my vantage point, but I can make out what he's doing and just about interpret his facial expressions.

His chest heaves in an exasperated sigh, so over pronounced I can make it out even from here. That must have been some meeting. I lean forward, resting my head on my hands as he grabs a bottle of water from the small fridge by his desk. He unscrews the cap and pours the crystal liquid into a tumbler, raising it to his lips. It's all so methodical and purposeful. I find his every move mesmerizing. I imagine the droplets of water perched on his full, pink lips, resting there, waiting for me. I can't take my eyes off him. He's done so well for himself, in that grand, rich looking office, sitting behind his mahogany desk, perched in his perfected position of power. He's strong and affluent and his office reaffirms that. My humble office, in stark comparison, could fit into his twice over at least. Truth be told, my office is more of a broom cupboard. I actually share it with multiple shelves of disorganised paperwork and stationary and occasionally an abandoned mop and bucket. The wilting office plant in the corner by the window is the closest thing to a decent conversation or interesting colleague I'll get all day.

I'm chewing my pen lid again, gnawing on the cheap blue plastic, semi-consciously hoping it doesn't explode and bleed blue ink all down my chin. How I'd love to build up the courage to go over there, to the bank. Oh, how I'd love to pluck up the confidence to surprise him. I could pretend I'm there to see him for business reasons - I'm sure I could make something up. I could do what all the lustful women do in the movies. I would slip on the most expensive, most extravagant underwear I could find, rolling the luxurious stockings over my knees and up my thighs, shrug on a mac just a few sizes too big so no one would know what I was concealing and cinch it in at the waist to cascade over my hips. I would allow myself in past his receptionist, pretending to be there as a representative of the charity—"a strictly business meeting," I'd assure her. It'd be quite easy, I think. I'd make my way in perched on my stilettos, close the door behind me and feel the heat and the chemistry burn as our eyes met over the polished mahogany of his desk. I could slip off the mac and walk seductively over and--

'Bye Sarah!'

I fling my head around and catch a glimpse of her face. She's been standing there the entire time, watching me staring at him. Was it obvious? Could she see what I was thinking? Was it that obvious - were my thoughts written on my face? I feel like she's walked in on me. Blood rushes up to my cheeks and I gather my things together in a frantic rush. I can feel how hot my face must look. I'm embarrassed to the point where I consider chasing after her, putting her straight, telling her I'm not feeling well, that maybe I've caught whatever has been going around the building lately. But she's already gone.

And though I can't even see the back of her head, I'm livid that I've let her get the better of me. I'm better than this. I'm better than her. I know it.

I hurl my bag over my shoulder and jog out of the office. The heels of my court shoes snag on the doorframe on my way out, and I shunt across the floor just about managing to retain my balance. Everything seems to be adding to my embarrassment, mounting up and making my face hotter and hotter. I'm overthinking it, overworking Ellis's reaction, I know I am, but I can't shift her smug face from my mind. She knows something, she must do. She knows what I'm up to. I grab the doorframe to steady myself, forcing air slowly into my lungs and slowly back out again. The rhythm of my breathing grounds me and soon the palpitations slide away. I remember him, his face and his smile and soon enough all annoyance at Ellis seems to drift from my shoulders. I'll be meeting him for the walk home.

I march the rest of the way out of the office, holding my head down and studying the floor. My cheeks are holding the heat of embarrassment, and I can feel eyes crawling over the back of my head as I leave. It only takes me a few minutes to get out of the building and onto the corner of the street. By the time I reach the coffee shop, I've caught up with him. His face is pulled quite taut. He's making no effort to hide the stress that the afternoon's meetings and appointments have clearly caused him. His expression is tired and worn, and I try to feel sorry for him, but all I feel is annoyance. My afternoon has been full of nothing but embarrassment, and he can't even pluck up the energy to ask me what's wrong.

'No, no. I've just had the afternoon from hell–you wouldn't believe it if I told you," I hiss under my breath. 'Ellis is really testing me; my job is less exciting than the Oxford dictionary, I've got no career prospects, I live in a hovel, and you can't even look me in the eye and ask me what's wrong? No, no. Never mind, it's too late now, anyway. I might as well be speaking to myself.'

Oh, and now he's making me feel guilty. I've had a slightly less than positive afternoon, and he looks like he might well be on the verge of a serious breakdown. I bite down on my bottom lip and stare, somewhat ashamedly, at the floor. I decide not to push him too far for details right now, but whatever it is that has happened clearly isn't good. I offer a warm smile of apology but it isn't readily received, so I leave it at that, and we walk home in silence. Not the uncomfortable kind, just the mutual kind. The kind that says, "I have had a really hard day, let's just enjoy each other's presence." I'm fine with that. Honestly.

We part ways at the corner of the road. I watch him walking away towards his high-end apartment, his head still hanging towards the floor. I watch for a few moments before turning the opposite direction towards my far more modest flat. The second I turn around it hits me again. The light, relaxed mood I'd experienced only minutes earlier seeped away, crashing to the floor and leaving behind a heavy, leaden lump in my chest. I should be used to this by now; my mood dips whenever I'm away from him. I've never discussed this with him–I think it would be too much pressure on our relationship. It's a physical, visual change, like a switch flicking over in my mind. Not just emotional, not something I can govern, but an uncontrollable wave that crashes over my torso. My chest drops, my eyebrows furrow into my forehead, my thoughts become greyer and more legato, kind of strung together and drawn out in a drunken daze. This is how I feel when I'm alone, surrounded by nothing but myself. I hollow out. I'm terrible at being lonely. As my energy levels sink, my mood is dragged down, plummeting, falling, and collapsing into lethargy. I drag my feet, my arms hanging limply by my side. It's not sadness; it's not a feeling–it courses through my whole body, dragging its way slowly through my arteries and pulling me down. It's like attempting every day, boring tasks whilst wading through water, heaving my limbs through feet of slick, thick treacle. It lingers the whole way home, forcing me to walk slower and suffer alone in the late afternoon sunlight.

Chapter Two

Liam. I've always fancied myself with someone called Liam. It sounds good; our names together, said quickly, so they sound like one word. Sarah and Liam. Liam and Sarah. I never thought it possible for me to truly be happy with someone like Liam, but here I am. Ecstatic. Overjoyed. I am the textbook definition of a happy person—content with life in all its glory. The obsessions I have with him, with his face, his voice, his personality–it's unrelenting. Love swallowed me whole without a word of warning, and here I am, besotted and unable to focus for the excitement that we'll be reunited in just a few hours. Being away from him makes my whole body throb and ache with the daunting reality of another night alone.

I force myself to follow the usual evening routine. I push aside the empty cartons in the kitchen, stab the plastic film on whichever microwave meal I plucked from the freezer and throw it into the orange-lit oven. I jab my finger into the grime-coated buttons and watch the green LED lights count down in preparation of my modest feast for one. I prefer to eat alone, really I would. I'm not a fan of small talk and forced conversation—of empty gestures and wasted words. I sit cross-legged on my armchair with a book and read whilst I eat. What better company can there be? Besides him, of course. I force the food down one chunk at a time, focusing on swallowing to draw my attention away from the taste. It's grey. The colour is grey. The taste is grey. I'm not a fan, but I wouldn't eat anything otherwise. I manage to eat the entire meal without even acknowledging the contents. I toss the packaging onto the windowsill and sit for a few minutes, staring into the darkness of the sitting room. I stare so hard dim colours start to crackle into my vision. These parts of my day feel so routine, so automatic that I no longer think about them. They're involuntary, each action slotting logically next to the previous one, each limb working and moving independently but somehow together. The apathy threatens to swallow me sometimes. It's there the whole time I'm alone, coiling up around my spine and pressing into my shoulders. I know I need to keep moving, to keep treading water. Without thinking, I find myself in the shower, dragging and scraping a loafer over my dry skin, to force myself to feel something, anything. Then I'm climbing into bed, kicking aside growing mounds of unwashed clothes. I'll read until the early hours, the words brushing across my eyes but never fully going in– I'm not a good sleeper, but I'm even worse at concentrating.

I've rolled onto my side, my hand flat underneath my pillow cradling my head. My room is pitch black except for the glowing green digits on my clock that read 3:01 a.m. I've stared at them for so long that they remain imprinted in my vision when I look away. This must be the fourth, maybe even fifth night in a row that I've been awake at this time, staring at the harsh green light in the heavy darkness of my room. The fatigue stings the rims of my eyes. I'm well acquainted with this insomnia, but it doesn't get any easier. I force my eyes closed against the darkness of my room, squinting tightly, allowing visions of him to fill the void in my mind. I imagine lying next to him, facing him with my eyes closed and listening to his breathing. I wait for him to exhale so I can catch his out breath and taste him. I consume him, smell him, breathe him in. I am consumed by him. I steady my breathing, listening to it whispering and rushing through my nostrils, rhythmic and meditative. I lay my hand on his cheek, brushing past the stubble on his chin. I feel myself slipping back and forth, in and out of consciousness, my mind so full of images of his face that there's no room for anything else. The weight of his body tips mine slightly, causing the springs in the bed to lightly moan and creak under the strain. His foot brushes up my calf, the coolness of it sending a shiver up my spine. The familiarity of him being there and the comfort of knowing I'm not alone finally allows me to drift off to sleep.

The sound of my alarm shakes me awake, the harsh beeping shrill against the silence. I open my eyes to find the other side of my bed empty and untouched. It takes me a while to work out why – a few minutes to distinguish whether last night happened, or if I imagined him in my bed.

I roll off the duvet, slipping on my shabby dressing gown and shuffle to the kitchen in a semi-conscious state. I rub my eyes, clumps of dried mascara flaking off onto my fingertips. I flick on a few lights as I go. The curse of being in a basement flat is that there is absolutely no natural light. It's almost like living in a casket. I'm sure that affects my mood when I'm home. I've read that houseplants help that kind of thing, but I can hardly look after myself. A plant would wither and die in the corner somewhere, unloved and ignored, shunned and neglected. I shed some light on my flat and remember why last night was absolutely, irrefutably a figment of my imagination. 100%, unquestionably in my head.

The harsh light of the cheap bulb casts the flat in a cold, clinical hue. A single hung photo perches at one end of the hallway - a snapshot of an old former friend and I at our university graduation tossing our mortarboards into the air.

'Good morning, Natalie,' I say, touching my fingertips to the frozen image. 'And how are we today? Still the same selfish bitch I so lovingly remember, I hope?'

I'm a completely different person from that day, from that time. Everything's changed about me. The photo makes me feel nauseous. Fake smiles, fake laughter, fake friends. I've not seen her since that day. She could be dead for all I know.

I take my hand away from the glass, leaving fingerprints behind in the condensation. As if living in a dingy, basement flat wasn't bad enough – the mould is next to impossible to get rid of. It hangs there, slick and shiny along the outer walls and ceiling. I scrape my fingernail along it, rolling and collecting black gunk under my fingernails. I'm sure it gets worse every time I scrub at it.

I flick the kettle on and go in search of a clean mug amongst the debris of used crockery and kitchen utensils. It's hard to keep on top of these things when you live on your own. It's hard to stay motivated to look after yourself, and I've always hated housework.

I'd never dream of bringing him back here, showing him the mess I live in. I could never welcome him to my front door, onto the stained doormat, and into the hallway, creeping with potentially hazardous spores. I don't know how exactly, but the flat makes me feel safe. No one else would ever want to come in, so I know I'm perfectly alone. And I'm more than happy for him never to find out.

I stumble through the kitchen, tea slopping over the edge of my mug and scorching my fingers. Something sticky has attached itself to my sock, balled up just under my toes. I scrape my foot on the coarse carpet, but the lodger won't budge. The tea's way too hot. I knew that before taking a sip, but I did it anyway, and, now, I've burnt the taste buds on the tip of my tongue.

'For God's sake, Sarah.' I raise my voice at the silence, kicking a stray makeup wipe across the floor. 'When, exactly, are you going to sort this place out? It's bloody disgusting.'

I drift through the flat, wasting time. I eventually get dressed, piecing together the day's outfit and drag a smear of makeup across my cheeks. I brush my hair, tugging at the knots and yanking the brush to the ends, scrunching at it and piling it on the top of my head. I pout at myself in the mirror, tilting my head to catch the best light and avoid the array of greasy fingerprints littering the glass.

'How can he not want this?' My breath sticks the glass, drifting across my face and towards my eyes. My eyes–God, they look awful. Bloodshot and dry and red and sad. The older I get, the more they seem to sink into my face, retreating from my cheeks. I force some peach gloss across my lips and focus my thoughts back to him. It's only a few minutes until

I'll be with him again and I can carry on living the life that I want, rather than being trapped in here. The thought of seeing him lifts my mood.

I turn away from the mirror and navigate my way out of my flat, stepping over the mountain of takeaway boxes and unread junk mail. The day is pleasantly warm, and I am optimistic.

I can see him already, leaving his apartment across the street, turning to lock the door, sliding his sunglasses onto his face in the bright, early spring sunshine. I stop in my tracks in awe of him. He looks impeccably smart; he must have some important meetings today. He's holding onto his briefcase, striding purposefully to the usual corner of the road where we meet and walk to work. I'm not actually the most talkative of people, and I remind myself how glad I am that he completely understands and accepts that. I think he likes the silence as much as I do. I rush to meet him, and we walk along the flower-lined pavement. I catch the unmistakable scent of his aftershave, masculine and strong. I try to breathe in enough of it to last me all day. We walk brusquely, swaying our arms in unison, matching each other's pace down to the last step. I sway my arms too vigorously and shiver as my hand brushes against his fingertips, quickly shoving it in my pocket out of embarrassment before he realises. Our feet meet the pavement together one last time before we part ways and walk the rest of the distance alone to our respective offices. We see each other off to work and go about our days. And just like that, just after seeing him for a matter of minutes, I'm back to being in a better place.

'Morning, Sarah. Good evening?' Ellis asks with a knowing glint across her face. She wears smug well. I can't let her think she's won again.

'You have no idea, Ellis. My evening was perfect; thank you for asking. Hot, steamy, everything I could possibly wish for and more,' I reply, dramatically loosening the collar of my blouse as I feign a hot flush. She squirms in front of me, a mixture of repulsion from my unnecessary divulgence of detail and desperate for more gossip to circulate in this drab office. She fumbles at my door, searching for the appropriate end to our brief encounter. I'm well aware that lying isn't very becoming, but fabricating the truth to make Ellis uncomfortable seems like a just cause to me. Besides, I don't really see it as lying so much as just bringing the timeline of our relationship forward. It's going to happen—it just hasn't happened quite yet, that's all.

'Oh and Ellis? You wouldn't believe how big—.'

'Oh! Really, Sarah? Not necessary,' she interrupts, her face flush with embarrassment. She turns on her heels and before I know it she's gone. She's so easy to wind up it's a shame not to tease her.

Chapter Three

One thing I do like about my job is how methodical and predictable it is. I'm never on the back foot. I know what to expect, and I know how to exploit that. Some may call it mundane and tedious, but I'm in control and that I like. Between the hours of 9 and 11 each and every weekday morning, excluding bank holidays and public holidays, I will be at my desk firing off replies to all queries received the night before. I'll go through the company's main inbox, delete junk and anything not relating to our services and organise my calendar for the day. Of course, my calendar is as in-sync with his as I can possibly get it. I'll drink one cup of strong tea, only ever made by me, and one glass of room temperature water. Routine is the spice of life. Everything runs smoothly and to plan, just as I like it. At about five to eleven, I gather my purse, lock my PC and sweep on my coat to walk to the coffee shop—of course, the same one every day—and share a coffee with my soul mate. Today is no exception.

I leave the office and within minutes arrive at the coffee shop. I purchase my usual latte from the barista, paying her the exact amount in loose change and take my usual seat away from the window with my usual latte and wait. I flick through my phone, have a look at some old photos, read some mundane news articles to pass the time. I wait.

And wait. He is never late. He values organisation and timekeeping just as much as I do. My watch reads 11:06, which means he is 6 minutes later than normal. Six minutes later than every other day I've met him. That's 6 minutes less time to spend with him. Maybe I knocked my watch in the night. I know I ought to remove it when I go to bed, but I always forget. I check the digital clock above the till. Seven minutes late. It flashes. Eight minutes late. Blood is rushing up to my cheeks, wrapping around my neck like a cheap nylon scarf. Nine minutes. Ten. I've been stood up. I can't believe it. I can't stomach the audacity. Everything has been perfect for so long, and now he's trying to destroy it? I can't lose control of this situation, not again. I'll sit here, finish my coffee like nothing has changed and walk back to my office, just the same as I did yesterday and the day before; the same as I will do tomorrow. This will change nothing.

I watch the minutes disappear. I keep glancing at the door expecting him to barrel through it in a rush, but he doesn't show. Maybe he's just in an important meeting, helping out a colleague, saving a starving child, rescuing a kitten from a nearby tree. There's bound to be a good reason for him not showing, but I can't help but feel completely betrayed. I've spent almost exactly 30 minutes sat here staring alternately at the clock and the door. My coffee is stone cold. The milk has formed a tepid layer of skin along the top, sticking to the sides of the tall glass. I can't drink it now – what a waste.

I compose myself, gather my things and nudge the now cold coffee across the table. I stand on shaky legs, feeling the eyes of everyone in the café on my back. They can sense my embarrassment. Every single person in here knows I was abandoned, again. I was the one that was left alone and they're judging me, pitying me as I walk out onto the street in silence, completely on my own. I need to walk slower to the office to properly compose myself and put on a face for the rest of the day.

'So, did you see him again? What do you even talk about every day? Don't you get bored with each other?'

Ellis is leaning against the doorframe leading into my office again, her arms crossed at her chest, her expression standoffish. Prying and gathering information on her daily sweep of the office, no doubt. Lying usually comes naturally when I'm face to face with her, but I truly can't stomach her attitude today. I lean my head on my hand, tilting my head and pursing my lips, locking my eyes onto hers.

'I did see him again, Ellis. We can talk for hours on end about nothing in particular–he's just that kind of guy–happy to be around me, you know? It's perfect. Even the silences are perfect.'

I spit my words out at her. The lies are there, and on paper, they might have worked, but my tone is venomous. I've let her know I'm upset, but I've also let her know she doesn't need to know anything about it. She doesn't have to know about my earlier heartbreak.

The lying is therapeutic, in a way. The words are effortless, even if they did act as a warning. There's nothing wrong with rolling over the cracks in life, filling in the blanks, ironing out a few creases. I'm merely editing what I feel other people need to know about me. And Ellis doesn't need to know anything.

She furrows her eyebrows but holds her tongue—I don't think she quite knows how to react. I hold her stare and witness her expression twist into something else entirely. Her head tilts to the side and her eyes widen. It's only as she turns away that I recognise the emotion—it's pity. She *pities* me. She feels sorry for me. I don't need her pity, her sadness. The heat is clambering up my neck again, closing in around my throat. I look down to see myself scratching and picking at the deep red varnish on my nails, flinging the tiny coils onto the carpet. They scatter all around my feet, dark red flecks spattering onto the cream carpet like shiny shards of blood. I don't need her pity—I don't need anyone's pity. The varnish has all but disappeared from my nails, but I carry on scratching at them anyway—harder and harder at the edges of my fingers until the skin starts to retract and peel. The computer screen swims in front of my eyes.

He fills every available inch of my mind, every available space in my head. Every thought of him, every memory of his face and his voice has crawled between each cortex of my brain, twisting around the base of my skull. He makes me anxious, passionate, and furious. He's wrapped his fist around my emotions, controlling them and controlling me. I can sense it now—I've become more aware. I've lost all ability to dictate my own mood, and I've given in to that fact. I've succumbed to his power over me. He has me right where he wants me. He's pulling the strings more than he'll ever know, and that needs to change.

My own free will is mine to command, not his—he just needs a gentle reminder, that's all. A reminder that I'm not going to be his puppet, not when I ought to be the one controlling his every movement. I thud the computer keys between thoughts, replying to untouched emails that I've left to stagnate in the bottom of my inbox. I've decided not to meet him for the walk home. I'll wait here for a few extra minutes to make sure I don't run into him. I can potter about here for a while; walk home at my own pace, with my own thoughts. I've always been independent, so there's no point changing now. Not for anyone.

The clock in the corner of my computer screen inches closer to the end of the day, the digits dragging closer to five. I want to leave. I want to run out onto the street to see him. I want to apologise for jumping to conclusions, to throw myself into his arms and smother my face into his neck and grovel. More than anything, I want to give in to my heart, but I make myself wait. I am in control of this; I will be in control of him. I wait until ten minutes past the hour and gather my things, nodding a polite goodbye to the handful of colleagues left in the office. I place one foot deliberately in front of the other to stop myself from sprinting into the street to see if he's still there. I rummage in my pocket, pulling out my phone. No missed calls, no new messages, no sign that he's even realised I'm not there. I flick through a few apps to waste some more time, and when my clock reads twelve minutes past, I give in and emerge onto the road.

It's quiet. Quieter than normal because of the few minutes grace the rest of the workers have had to get home. I throw a cursory glance up to his window to check that he's not still there. The opaque blinds block his room off to onlookers, but I can't see any signs of moving shadows, so I assume he's left.

I walk past the supermarket, past the coffee shop, past the row of tall Victorian townhouses, past the park full of children and families and laughter. And laughter. Laughter that gets louder and shriller the closer I get to it. Such a sense of forced happiness. It all makes me angry, this pretence that we can be anything but bitter and miserable. The noise rises and scratches against my skull, teasing the silent rage I've held down for the day, testing its patience. What I'd do to silence that sound of happiness, what I'd give to suffocate it. I walk faster until I can see the entrance to my basement flat. Every ounce of the day's energy is sucked out of me down those stairs, out of my chest, plunging through the front door. The door that has been there since the day I moved in all those years ago. Painted in layers of thick black gloss which curls away at the edges - number '47'. Only the '7' has lost a screw and now hangs upside down. At least it's down the stairs in the basement so no one can see it - no one but me. My feet thud down the concrete stairs, passing the empty lager cans that have been lovingly abandoned by another lodger from the floor above me.

As I approach my front door, I realise something has changed. There's more movement and noise than usual, more hustle and bustle. There's a 'To Let' sign jutting out of the ground at an angle next to the rusty washing line. I hang back a few moments and watch a young couple heave their remaining few belongings into the back of a removal van. They look happy. He's smiling at her, and she is smiling back. I flick my eyes over what appears to be a swollen stomach and his hand resting on her shoulder - that explains a lot. You wouldn't want to raise a child in this block of flats. I have never once spoken to these people, not welcomed them with baked goods or made small talk on my way out in the mornings. I've never made a point of speaking to any of the other tenants in this building, actually. There are only two other flats right at the top of the house, and their inhabitants are as private as I am. They're so quiet I can't guarantee that they live there anymore. I stand and watch for a few seconds longer, jealous of their happiness and their easy, normal lives. I imagine the excitement they must be feeling, heaving their entire life packed up in suitcases and brown cardboard boxes into the back of a van. Rolling and wrapping their trinkets in yesterday's headlines, slotting them next to each other in boxes like fragments of memories they don't want to forget, but eventually will anyway. They're ready to start their next chapter. They slam the back of the van shut and climb into the front, ready to drive away.

I turn back around to face my home and fumble around in my bag for my key. I force the door through a growing mountain of takeaway leaflets and adverts that have piled on the floor. They've been there for as long as I can remember, forming their own small mountain of shiny paper. I still can't muster the energy to clear them up, so they live to see another day. The paper only allows the door to open a couple of feet or so, leaving me no choice but to squeeze myself through into the hallway, the door springing shut behind me with a groan of relief. My, what my mother would say if she could see my humble abode. I laugh out loud in my empty flat, the sharpness in my voice cracking the silence. She doesn't know I live here. She doesn't even know if I'm still in the country. I cut all ties with my family years ago after they lost interest in me. After they realised that no amount of *sessions* would make me, or them, feel any better. My mother tried, bless her soul. Honestly, she really was so innocent in it all. I caught myself, just then, saying 'was,' as if my mother was dead. I don't think she is, though I doubt my family would bother to tell me if anything had happened. So yeah, why not? To make this easier for all involved, let's assume she's dead. My mother *was* so innocent. She thought the best in everyone; saw the light in everyone's personalities. Even mine. And we all know what a mistake that proved to be.

'Oh mother, where art thou?'

I shout it aloud into the living room, kicking a used take away box across the stained carpet. Low and behold, I'm alone. What a surprise. My bag lands on the floor with a thud, and I prop myself against the doorframe of the kitchen.

It is disgusting in here. Not what civilised people call disgusting. I don't mean there a few dishes scattered on the surfaces or a stray oven tray with the meal from the night before left to linger. I mean *disgusting* and I'm not one to exaggerate. It's filthy - vile. Plates are stacked on the sides, a few on the floor, in the sink - covering every spare inch, every available surface – a vast city of leaning crockery. Many of them have started to grow mould. A few of them started that process weeks ago and are now coated in a thick green-brown fur. I'm sure it must smell in here, but I suppose I'm used to it by now. I can't tell any more. Thinking about it, I can't remember the last time I bothered to use a plate. I've resorted to buying microwave meals in bulk. I cook them in their packets and eat them straight out of the plastic with disposable cutlery I pocket from the Marks and Spencer's down the road. The packets never actually find their way to the bin and have gathered in a tumbling heap next to my favourite armchair in the living room. In between the packets and on top of the packets and beside the packets are my old collection of ashtrays, spilling with stale cigarette ends and silver-grey fag ash. Not a single cigarette has touched my lips in weeks. It's not a case of habit or addiction; it's occasional self-destruction.

I fall into the armchair, tagliatelle and plastic fork in hand, and fold my legs underneath me. I eat and I think about the day. I also think about yesterday and about tomorrow and the day after and what joys that will bring to my life. It still hurts, him standing me up like that, but now I'm back in my flat and back to my usual grey personality, lacking a sense of purpose. I feel comfortable again. Unhappy but comfortable and safe and relatively unsurprised that he stood me up. But I'm sure it was a one-off. He'll be there tomorrow. And if he isn't, I'll go and find out why. I can make sure it doesn't happen again.

I twist some slimy, beige pasta around the fork, piling it into my mouth, ignoring the taste as best as I can. Even the way I'm eating is angry. I can't shake myself out of it. My temper has wrapped itself around my heart, its tendrils spreading over my chest and around my neck, weaving in between my ribcage. I will make absolutely sure no one ever makes me feel this way. Not again. I hate him for it. I hate myself for letting him get to me this much.

I finish the grey matter masking itself as pasta and fling the packaging on top of the closest pile, watching as the fork falls out of the packet and bounces to the floor. I won't pick it up.

Why bother? I sit cross-legged for potentially hours–I don't check the time–silently stewing with anger and wondering why I'm not good enough this time around. What did I do wrong this time? I should go to bed, but I can't bring myself to move, to shower, to catch a glimpse of my pathetic, lonely face in the mirror. So I sleep where I am, screwed up in an angry ball in the armchair, chain-smoking and swearing at myself under my breath until exhaustion finally claims me and I give up and fall to sleep.

I wake early. My joints are stiff from sleeping in such an awkward position and pins and needles prickle the soles of my feet. I look at my watch, which I forgot to remove again last night. It's nearly 8:00. I heave myself out of the chair and pull my body into a standing shape against its will. The pins and needles spread angrily over my thighs and into my hands. I shed my clothes as I walk awkwardly to the bathroom and clamber into the shower, which is no cleaner than the kitchen. I twist the hot tap, limescale flaking off onto my fingers and dusting the bottom of the bathtub. The hot water scalds me, but I don't turn down the temperature. I scrub myself to get rid of the grimy feeling the flat gives me, scraping a loofa hard into my flesh until it leaves bright red grooves and scratch marks against my pale skin. I stand facing the hot water for a few moments, concentrating on each individual droplet bouncing from my face. I wander through the rooms of my flat naked, slowly getting dressed and scrape my hair back up onto the top of my head. I don't eat. I don't bother. I don't see the point. I smear some old, clotting foundation over my cheeks and under my eyes to hide the growing grey bags. I haven't let go of what he did to me yesterday, but I'm not angry anymore. I'm still disappointed, but his disrespect for me has just made me feel numb and cold. That's the last time I play the victim.

I catch sight of myself on my way towards the front door. I look ill and thin; the lines of my face are protruding and making my eyes and cheeks look sallow. I can't bear to look any longer, so I leave my hovel of a flat and enter the real world, leaving the heaps of mould and take-away leaflets behind me for another day of pretence and polite falsifications.

He's there, on the corner. I can see him already. I thought seeing him would make me feel worse; I thought it would deepen my already black mood. But my anger at the previous day immediately lifts off my shoulders, drifting away into the sky above me—a black cloud lifting off my chest and floating off into the outskirts. I'm almost more annoyed that seeing him has made me drop my guard. He's turned me too soft. He smiles, and I return the expression without thinking. He makes me feel so euphoric, so ecstatic, that I suddenly remember what it is to be alive. We meet in the usual spot and walk together in blissful peace. I was worried we might argue, but I don't have the energy to hold onto the negativity and anger from yesterday, and he seems happy enough to start afresh. He's wearing a clean, pressed white shirt and the usual strong, masculine cologne. His cufflinks throw the bright sun around as he swings his arms in time with mine and I'm back to thinking he's perfect almost instantly. We walk in unison, our feet hitting the concrete together and before I know it, I sit back at my desk, wondering desperately what I was so livid about just hours before.

Chapter Four

I bump into Ellis in the kitchen. She's making coffee for herself and a handful of our colleagues, though never me. I always make my own. I grin at her, and she offers an arguably genuine smile back.

'Morning Sarah. You look nice today,' she says, still grinning.

'Oh, thanks, Ellis.' I don't quite know how to take the compliment. It's very rare that Ellis and I have any kind of genuine conversation, and I can't help but let my guard slam up in front of me in case this is just some kind of game to her. I went to school–I experienced being routinely picked last and being at the receiving end of the other girls' jokes. I know what I should be looking out for in Ellis' face. So I'll take the compliment, but I'm wary.

'A few of us are having a get-together Saturday night. Do you want to come? It's just at my place, just a few friends,' she asks without peering up from her tea. 'We might order pizza, watch a film, drink some wine–the usual.'

This is the first time Ellis has ever asked this kind of question. I search around frantically for an excuse, any reason to say no. I'm happy for the genuine conversation, but seeing Ellis outside of work? I don't know if I am able to fake 'Work Sarah' outside of work hours. I stammer, desperately wracking my brains for a viable lie but it isn't happening. Maybe I should go. Maybe it would be good for me. It would help pass the time whilst I'm not with him, at least.

'Sure, I think I'm free. Sounds good.' My mouth has answered before I can come up with a convincing excuse not to accept. I smile at her. She smiles at me. It's not nearly as awkward as I make it sound.

'Great. I'll email you my address,' she says as she walks off to her corner of the office. She places her hand on my shoulder as she leaves, smiling on her way out. I instinctively flinch in response to her fingers making contact with my blouse, and I hope to God she didn't realise. Maybe we're turning a corner.

I finish making my coffee and walk it back to my desk. I'm still stunned by her attitude towards me–still shocked that she's asked me into her personal space. Part of me worries that this is a *Carrie* style set up. That I'll arrive at her apartment and it's all just been a game, a way to lure me into a false sense of security and watch me fall, rolling around her floor covered in pig's blood and the like.

I sit down, placing my coffee to the right of my old, worn keyboard. I nudge the mouse, watching the computer as the light starts to spread across the screen. I hit the keyboard, my hands remembering the keys that make up my username and password before my mind does. I do the usual–I check emails, I send emails, I file emails, I delete emails, I type up minutes from the meetings the day before, and I send them as an email. I successfully make myself look considerably busier than I ever actually am. I look busy and productive when realistically I'm spending my time thinking about him. I flit my eyes down to his window, but he's not there yet. His office stands empty with the blinds open but no sign of his face.

I'm in love with him. It's unmistakeable, the feeling of euphoria when I see him and the deep, hollow feeling of rejection when he misses a single cup of coffee with me. It must be love. Everything about him is perfect; what else could the feeling be? I have felt this way before, I think, but this is different, stronger, and more intense. I'm excited beyond words at the thought of seeing him later. Seeing him back at our usual spot, where I'll be waiting for him. I've got the best news to tell him, that I've finally fallen in love with him. He'll be thrilled when I tell him, I know. He's been waiting for me to say it, I think. I can see it in his eyes, in the way he holds himself around me. He's just waiting for me to say it so he can say it back.

The morning drags as I think of nothing but his face, his lips, his eyes. Eleven finally rolls around, and I rush out of the office in a daze. I can't wait to see him, to tell him how I feel and finally move our relationship to the next level. I float through the office doors and to my usual spot in the coffee shop, cradling my latte. Today I've treated myself to a slice of carrot cake. It's nothing too fancy, but it's something to mark the occasion in my mind. I sit, picking at the icing, stirring the frothed milk in my coffee.

I find myself waiting again. It's only a few minutes past eleven. That's nothing. There's no need to panic–no cause for alarm. It's only a few minutes. His meeting has clearly overrun, and I'm not worrying. I look down at the table, at my fingers furiously drumming on the pale wood. The frustration is creeping up on me again. The anxiety is back, the doubts that he feels the same way, the obvious reality that I love a man that can't love me back. I try to bat the thoughts away, but they're resilient. Where is he now? How dare he–again? The blood is flooding up through my neck when I finally see his face through the glass panel in the door. Calm down, Sarah, he's right there. Just a few minutes late. Probably stuck in an important meeting or something. He's not as lucky as me; he can't get up and leave his office whenever he feels like it. There he is, just sorting his jacket out ready to come inside and sit down. He's smiling. His smile is stunning - so peaceful and genuine. I'm staring at him again, losing myself in his eyes. The happiness washes over me in waves as the dopamine hits my mind. Pure euphoria. He's taking slightly longer than normal to come inside. I crane my neck up from my table. I can see him. I can see the back of his head, the small wisps of dark hair gathered at the base of his neck. I can see his crisp white shirt and his phone hanging in his right hand at the side of his body. I can see–I see a woman's hand, small and delicate, resting on his shoulder. He's not flinching; he's not pushing her hand away and correcting her behaviour in the way I would if another man was touching me. He's happy to leave it there.

It dawns on me. He's *with* someone else. His hand–his hand is on her cheek, stroking it, holding her face. He's leaning in to–no, no I can't. I can't watch this. He's with someone else. He's going to *kiss* someone else. I can't watch. It's torture. I'm not angry; I'm incredibly upset, but not angry. Not yet. He's bringing her in here. He's bringing this filthy woman into the café that we always meet at. I can't stomach how audacious this is. This is our spot, and he is bringing someone else here. He didn't even break up with me. What did I do? They look sickly sweet together, holding hands, staring into each other's eyes. I can feel myself staring, burning hot tears pooling in my eyes, threatening to expose me. I can't pull my eyes away from them. The blood is rushing back through my neck. My heart is racing, and my blood pressure must be dangerously high by now. Oh god, they look so happy–I might vomit. I'm stunned into silence, stunned and frozen to the spot where I sat. I need to leave; I need air.

I grab my things in one shaking hand, shoving the latte towards the edge of the table and sloshing coffee over the sides and onto the floor. I can't stay here for another minute. I hurtle myself out of the coffee shop, barging past the other occupied tables, bumping into other customers and knocking coffees and cakes left, right, and centre.

'Alright, love, watch where you're going!'

Someone yells at me. I hardly even hear it. The yell is an echo at the back of my mind, an attempt to tug me back to reality.

I realise all too late that I'm sobbing–hot, embarrassed, betrayed tears. I feel certain that he's seen me. It was my choice to let him in, and he destroyed me. I explode onto the path outside the café, tears spilling over my cheeks. My knees buckle as I throw my weight down onto the nearest bench and let my head collapse onto my knees.

I love a man that doesn't love me back. Not only does he not love me back, he loves someone else. I saw the way he was looking at her. How could he? I can't understand it. I'm trying to process it, but the more I try, the more I go back to imagining the two of them in there, sat opposite each other, staring into each other's eyes and whispering sweet nothings at one another. I feel sick. So many weeks and months we had together, wasted. So many things I shared with him. I trusted him, and now this.

I know how ridiculous it is to torture myself like this, but it's impossible to keep the images of them out of my mind. Every time I blink and close my eyes, it's like I'm back in the cafe, faced with seeing the two of them together. Visions of their lips joining together, their hands interlocked. Her face nestled close to his where mine ought to be. I'll kill her.

The tears are relentless, splashing from my cheeks and onto my shirt. I can't go back to the office like this. I can't even think of the office. I don't care about my job; I can't face Ellis, I can't stare at my computer all afternoon while that *woman* is in there manipulating him, convincing him that he loves her and not me. How dare she. How dare she sink her teeth into him. He's not the guilty one here - I know that. It's her. He's so loving and kind and easily led. I need to get her away from him.

I grab my bag from the floor by the bench and run home. I need to be alone, in my flat, surrounded by my belongings, nestled amongst the rubbish and mess where I feel safe. The streets are filling with workers leaving their offices for lunch, and I weave in and out of busy pockets of people. Sweat gathers on my forehead as I run up to my flat in the bright sunshine. I force my way into the flat and collapse amongst the takeaway menus on the floor, kicking the door closed behind me. I scream, I cry, I scream again.

Stay there, Emily! Don't move!

What have I done to deserve this? Again? My chest burns with anger. I'm agitated and on edge and desperate to know the reason why this sort of thing keeps happening–why it insists on happening to me. I can almost see it again, the crumpled, lifeless body.

Please Grandma, what is it? What are you doing? What are you hiding?

How can someone be so unlucky?

I scratch the palms of my hands, raking at the skin to try and bring my mind back to reality. I need to drag myself away, back to the present day. I cry, hysterical, jerking floods of tears, loud, animal-like sobs. I can feel the spit strung out between my lips, frothing at the corners of my mouth and draping from my teeth. I must look like some kind of ravenous, rabid animal, cowering on the floor behind my door screeching and screaming in anger. I punch the wall, lunging my body and fist into the plaster and let out a yell of pain. My knuckles connect with the plaster. They crack under the force, sending a burst of red-hot pain shooting up and blossoming over the back on my hand. I need to punish myself for this–I need to make sure I can still feel. Any sane person would have cowered and held their hand to their chest, rocking on the floor in fits of agony. But I don't give up so easily. I know I haven't felt enough yet; I haven't put myself through enough just yet. I pull the same arm back, holding it high behind my ear like an archer and send it sailing through the air back into the wall. It crunches loudly. My knuckles are torn from their cradles and slide back in with a sickening pop. I scream out in pain, grabbing my hand to my chest and rocking myself to try to calm my heart rate. My whole hand has been swallowed by fire. The pain licks up my forearm and brushes just shy of my elbow. I feel sick. The pain is incredible.

'He doesn't love me.' I spit the words across the floor, phlegm flying from my lips and hanging from my chin. 'I love him. But he doesn't care.' My breathing is fractured and jerks in and out between my sobs and whimpers. 'And I'm not allowed to care anymore.'

And yet here I am, sitting on my floor in excruciating, self-inflicted pain, screeching and yelling, rolling around and cradling my bloodied, broken hand. I give up. I lie down amongst the mattress of takeaway leaflets, staring at the cobweb-covered ceiling and accept that nobody could ever love someone like me. I was made to be alone. He deserves to be happy, and I should just let him be.

I stand up on weary legs, a hollow emptiness washing over me. I hold myself against the wall as the anger and tears leave my body. They leave nothing behind except a bout of nausea and a slightly giddy sensation. My insides have been raked and scraped from their cradle and replaced off-kilter, leaving a wave of the deepest, darkest depression. I feel it as my body shifts to autopilot, as I stop letting myself feel anything but the pain in my hand. I give way to my body and allow my feet to take control. I have developed a kind of muscle memory, and my limbs seem to know my evening routine better than I do. I don't know what time it is; I just know I need this day to be over. I walk to the fridge, grab the first meal that is facing me, stab the clear film a few times and shove it into the uncleaned microwave. I know I need to let the office know where I am–I know how dodgy it would look if I just disappeared from another job. I also know I can't face calling them. They'd hear through the lies, I think. I grab my phone from my back pocket and hastily put together an email detailing possible food poisoning and how I'd be away from the office for a while to recover. No one questions food poisoning.

The microwave makes a dull, sad *ding* to indicate that my low calorie, low nutrition, low flavour meal is safe to eat–at least scientifically. I grab it with my uninjured hand and robotically manoeuvre my way into the living room, collapsing in a heap in the armchair. I lean out of the chair and fish a used, plastic fork from an old microwave tray that's perching on the windowsill. The remains of a meal from a few nights ago cling to the plastic prongs, reminding me of my less than ideal lifestyle. I eat, alone with my thoughts, but not really thinking of anything, concentrating on the small, hard potatoes, focusing meditatively on chewing and swallowing but not actually tasting. I eat most of the food, despite its overwhelming blandness and I curl up in the corner of the armchair like a wounded animal, clutching my hand to my chest. The pain is unreal, but I convince myself that it is wholly justified. I deserve to hurt. I deserve to be in pain for the things that I've thought about him – the things I've wished upon him. It's not his fault; I know that now. It's her fault, whoever she is. I feel sorry for him in a way. I feel bad that he's been so easily led astray by a pretty, blonde airhead like her. I'll get him back, because I love him and I still need to tell him that. He needs to hear it, because I need to hear it back. I force some cocodamol down my dry throat to dull the excruciating pain that is still throbbing between my knuckles and over the back of my hand. I wonder what Liam would say if he could see me now. I'm thankful he can't. I look a state. Curled up in the corner of the sofa, hanging my head in shame. The tears are still coming, but they are no longer hysterical. They trickle over my cheeks and, though I can feel them, warm and wet against my weathered skin, the only emotion I can distinguish is emptiness. They are tears of nothingness—tears of hollowness and tears of exhaustion.

Chapter Five

I stir early, awoken by the throbbing that has wrapped itself around my hand and wrist like an iron glove, piercing and scraping at my nerves and tendons. I look down at what I've done to myself. It doesn't look great, but I think it'll heal itself. I won't go to a hospital unless I have absolutely no choice. The back of my palm has bloomed into a deep purple flourish of bruises, broken up with hints of green and blue. The bruises are deep, and my hand is swollen. It looks strangely beautiful, despite the pain. It's like I've placed droplets of ink into a shallow pool of water and let the dark purples and rich blues flood and bleed into one another. It wraps itself all over my hand, lacing through the gaps between my knuckles and fingers and around my wrist. It certainly doesn't look healthy. I try to clench my hand into a fist and wince as the flesh threatens to split across my knuckles. I walk to the bathroom and grab a bandage from an old first aid kit. I wrap it tightly around my hand. I'm not sure how to wrap it properly, so I just thread the bandage around my wrist and between my thumb and forefinger, pulling it tightly to give it support. I wince as the rough material brushes the bruising. It's hot to the touch, and my skin is pillowy and inflated, like there's too much flesh being trapped by my skin. Once I've managed to wrap it as best I can, I bring myself to look in the mirror. What I see is almost as disturbing as my injuries. My face is puffy and red from a night of almost constant crying and very little worthwhile sleep. My eyes are raw and bloodshot, outlined in a deep pink hue, which makes them look like they protrude from my face. Greasy, oily hair hangs on top of my head, a few strands dangling onto my cheeks. My lips are chapped and slightly bleeding where I've neglected to use Vaseline over the winter months. I look unloved. I look neglected and abused. What a sight.

I walk to the kitchen and take a swig of cold milk, straight from the bottle. I look around at the state of the place that I call home. It's not often that I actually *see* how I live anymore. I'm so used to it, I've become blind to the problems.

The kitchen is revolting, the living room a dark hole full of empty microwave meal packages and mugs and the bedroom is not much better. The bedroom is hardly ever used, except to get dressed in the mornings and sleep if I make it as far as the bed. There are clothes piled high all over the floor, dirty and clean mixed together. The bed hovers amongst the laundry, unmade and covered in dirty, stained off-white bed sheets. Every window is dripping with condensation, even at this time of year. The windows all face an outer wall, so they only let in a trickle of light that casts awkward shadows on the rubbish piled up in the dingy basement flat.

Life has been this way for as long as I can remember—so long that it's now natural to be surrounded by debris and mould. How can I expect him to care for me the same way that I care for him when I live like this? There's not a single part of me that thinks he'd ever want to come here. I can imagine him now, living in some posh, upmarket apartment, surrounded by class and cleanliness. She's probably there, laughing about me, pitying me, draping her long, slender limbs over his body. I can feel them together, her twisting the dark curls of hair behind his ears with her delicate fingers. Her breath tickles his neck as she whispers to him, teasing him, making him believe he's happy with her.

As I'd begun to drift off, it came to me - the way I'll show him how much he means to me, the way I can prove that I'm serious about our relationship. I'll ask him to move in with me.

It happened as consciousness started to fail me. A heavy fog began to seep over my mind—a mixture of total exhaustion and the generous dose of painkillers I'd taken to dull the pain and throbbing in my hand. As the fog descended and my eyelids dropped against my face, I realised that I needed him here to love him the way he needs to be loved. The idea seemed perfect as I nodded off and dreamt, but it quickly shattered as my eyes opened, adjusting to the dingy light of the living room. There's no way I could bring him here, not with my flat looking like an abandoned homeless shelter that even the squatters had given up on.

I need to change. This needs to change.

I heave myself out of the armchair, unfolding my legs from under my torso. The sudden shift in weight sends a flurry of pins and needles scurrying across my limbs. I tiptoe to the bathroom as lightly as possible, trying my best not to disturb my prickling legs and feet. The purple bruising has grown fiercer overnight. It covers my whole hand, deep and dark and indigo. One nail is blackening so fast it might not last the whole day. It needs re-wrapping, I'm sure of it. With my uninjured hand, I rummage in the drawer for a fresh bandage. The coarse fabric brushes across my swollen skin, pain jolting over the back of my hand and shooting up to my elbow. I throw some painkillers down my dry throat against a wave of nausea, struggling to swallow the dusty pills. My face is grey and sallow and beaten down–it's almost unrecognisable, staring back at me through the dust-lined mirror. I tug and pull at my cheeks, encouraging some colour to come back to my expression. I need to shake myself out of this mood, I know. I need to work out how to win him back and make sure I don't let him slip away again. I need to show him how much I love him, how serious I am about us. I need to remind him how much I want this to work and how I want to start a family with him. I won him the first time around–I can do it again.

It's time to sort out my flat, time to show him that I can be the one he is in love with and time for him to move in with me. My chest billows with a sense of confidence as the plan forms in my mind. It will all go perfectly; I can feel it.

'I love him,' I say to my reflection. He loves me just as much; he just doesn't know it as strongly as I do yet.

The kitchen is overwhelmingly dirty. A sickly scent of mould hangs in the air amongst the heaps of rubbish and unwashed crockery. I can't bear to look at it anymore, not without feeling repulsed at myself. I grab a black bag, shoving it under the armpit of my injured arm and hand. Handfuls of empty food packets and fistfuls of sticky, tacky plastic containers make their way into the sacks. Piles and piles of dirty, grimy packaging lined with green fuzz that brushes against my fingertips. The bags fill up quickly and line the hallway. Bag after bag after bag waiting to be dumped. Each bag is full of empty meals for one and a complete disregard for personal hygiene.

Virtually nothing is salvageable. My belongings have been engulfed and swallowed by damp and mould, their musty smell puffing out into the room in tiny grey clouds when touched. A few books can be saved, but besides that, there's no longer anything in any corner of the flat that would give away an inch of my personality.

The empty rooms stand, imposing, mocking my lack of character. The living room no longer resembles a graveyard of empty microwave meal packets but instead stands completely hollow, grey and cold. The carpet has worn thin and patchy; it's covered in dark, grimy scabs–scars left from mould and a lack of natural light. The windowsills are littered with rings from old coffee cups. My lone armchair sits in the empty cube with a small, chipped table tucked under one side. The dining table across the other side of the space is scuffed, but stands defiant by the door, as if it's survived the onslaught. There's no other furniture. I never saw the sense in buying anything that wasn't essential, but now the chair seems to hover on the balding carpet, cowering in the corner of the room. I've never bothered with a bookcase, or a lamp or television or home phone or trinkets. I always come straight home from work, have food and sleep. I have never worked out the value of wasting money on home comforts that I just don't feel are necessary.

I'm not a material person, but the reality of owning nothing; of having no value attached to anything I can call my own, presses on my chest. I've had an entire lifetime and made no impact on the world, no impression even on the place I'm supposed to call home. If I were to die today and someone found this room, this flat, there'd be no indication of who lived here. There'd be no sign or clue to figure out my personality, no photographs of genuine loved ones, no tacky souvenirs from cheap all-inclusive holidays in the sun. There is literally nothing here. I have always been alone, and this flat has made sure of it.

My family doesn't know I'm here. They don't know where I am, whom I'm with or who I even am anymore. I was very careful when I left - slipped out in the dead of night when they were least expecting it. I left everything behind except my money and a rucksack with a few essentials and I did everything in my power to make sure they'd never find me. By the time they realised I was gone for good and not just on another mindless bender, it was too late. It's very hard for a missing person to be found if they really want to stay hidden. I'm sure they eventually realised my absence was for the best. I have no doubt that it was better for them, so I hope they stopped looking. They finally stopped trying to save me. After years of me begging and pleading to be left alone, they finally stopped trying.

My family doesn't even know my name.

Chapter Six

I should buy a rug, I think. I've always fancied one—one of those big, oversized Turkish affairs that make the owner look richer and more intellectual than they actually are. And maybe a bookcase or two, something to fill the space. That way I can cover up the worst of the floor without having to have someone come and fix a new carpet, and I can look well travelled. I never want anyone else to come in here besides Liam and I. This will be our safe haven. It will be perfect and homely and full of love. And no one need know either of us is ever here.

I spend the next 6 or so hours scrubbing every inch of the flat one-handed. I scrape away the grime running between the tiles in the bathroom, chip away the lime-scale coating the underside of the taps and drench the shower in bleach until the smell burns my nostrils and eyes and threatens to swallow my vision in a migraine. How I ever managed to get clean in this room is beyond me.

The kitchen is somehow worse. Lifting the rubbish and ruined plates and mugs reveal the real issue underneath. Every spare inch of surface is covered in mould-coated crockery and inundated with dark green and white-flecked spores. There's an old bin bag hidden in the corner. A light layer of dust coats the top of the bag - I can't tell how long it has been sat there for. I lift it to move it out of the way, holding it suspended in the air as it drips with some unknown, cloudy coloured juice. The smell is unreal–a putrid, fermented ammonia oozing from the black plastic. A cluster of shiny white maggots tumble from the opening in the bag, and I chuck it down in disgust, fighting back a lump of sick in my throat. My toes curl up in my socks in repulsion as I grab hold of it at arm's length and run it through the hallway, dumping it on the floor outside the front door. The thought of the larvae crawls across my skin, my left hand instinctively rushing to cover my mouth as I choke back vomit. I wretch and shiver at the memory of the bugs' tiny cream bodies spilling onto the floor. I slide some shoes on for protection and drown the kitchen in Dettol until I can only just breathe. I slam the door on the kitchen, trapping the ammonia and gas inside, just to make sure there are no other critters scuttling around.

The bedroom isn't as horrific as the rest of the rooms in the flat. It's messy, but by no means grimy. The bed-sheets are by far the worst thing to deal with. I can't remember the last time they were changed, or I bothered to wash them. They were cream, but they're now littered with little islands of off yellow and beige, like an old tea stained map. I bundle them up and shovel them in another bin liner, searching the cupboards for a makeshift sheet for the night. Everything in the box at the bottom of the wardrobe is clammy and dewy. There's definitely nothing worth putting on the mattress, so the contents of the box follow the bedding into the bin bag.

The springs and slats of the old frame creak as I sit heavily on the edge of the bed for a breather. So much needs to change in here to make it warm and feel like a home. Hell, I need to change to make this place feel like a home.

'Where to start?' I murmur into the empty silence.

I can't bring myself to clean anything else today. I've been at it for hours, scrubbing and clearing, sweeping out any modicum of my character I had left and dumping it into black sacks. I'm exhausted. I feel as empty as the flat I'm standing in. The door to the kitchen cracks open just a few inches, letting the bleach seep out into the hallway in choking, bitter tendrils. The acrid smell doesn't let up, but at least I know it's clean now.

The armchair catches the weight of my body as the exhaustion starts to set in again. I sit for a while, floating in the emptiness of the living room. It's vast and hollow and has a slight dusty tang now I've cleared everything out. Everything feels vaguely familiar but strange and new at the same time, as if I'm looking at the place with fresh eyes but with constant déjà vu. The whole flat is clinical, empty, but the clutter still sits behind my eyes, fogging up my vision and concentration. It's hard not to take in every disgusting detail of the flat now I can finally see it clearly.

I walk through the flat slowly, exaggerating every footstep, fanning my toes out onto the stained, patchy carpet. The mattress perches on top of the divan, sinking and sagging, the floor grey in the dim light. I grab a thinning blanket from the bedroom and head back to the armchair to curl up and sleep. Fading light fills the room, casting stark shadows and grey hues across the walls. I sit, perched in my armchair, swimming in an empty, carpeted box. It's so much colder now the room is empty. I can see the breath spilling out of my nostrils in front of me, swirling in tendrils like smoke dancing in the air.

I wake with a start in the carpeted casket, wriggling my fingers and toes against the cold air. The room smells dank and strangely of soil, a lingering reminder of the mould and damp and weeks old food packaging. I fumble in my mind for a memory of what has happened. A few seconds pass as the realisation and recollection of the previous day settles in. It's Saturday. Yesterday was Friday. Yesterday was the day I made a decision to change the way I live and today is the day that I continue that decision. Today is the day that I venture into town to make my flat look convincingly like the home it's never been. I've been from room to room taking note of what I need, what it will take to make this place look like it's been lived in and loved and treated as a home. I know what I need to get, what I need to do—now I just need to do it. I catch myself breathing heavily at the thought of crowds and screaming children and hoards of people rushing through the streets like swarms of bees. I'm more suited to doing things alone, and the idea of being thrust into a crowd makes me nervous. But it's a sacrifice I need to take to move on. The anxiety threatens to close in around my throat. I can't let this stop me from changing things for the better—for both of us. I grab a glass of cold water, forcing myself to swallow and focus on the cool liquid in my mouth, in my throat. I think of him, of his face, of his smile, of the way he makes me feel, of the security he gives me. I'm making the right decision.

I march out of the flat, dragging the evening's hoard of bin bags behind me. The black plastic stretches and fades to grey, threatening to shred against the weight of the contents as I heave them into the skip so helpfully abandoned by the flat above. The daylight is bright and glaring and makes my eyes water, but at least the streets are reasonably quiet. A few people are going about their business, a few pairs holding hands, another staring at their phone, the odd child littering the pavement. It's like they've all been muted, quietly walking in the sun.

I head to the nearest department store and begin filling a trolley with soft furnishings, cushions, photo frames, bathroom supplies, cooking utensils–all those things you take for granted but that I've never been bothered to own. Literally everything you would need to purchase when buying your first place to live, your first place to call home. Only I've been living in my flat for the last four years and had never bothered wasting my money on anything that would make me feel at home. It's alien, being in here, surrounded by young mums buying up cushions and throws and paper flowers and trinkets. It's all so superficial, but it feels good in a way, to finally be buying it all, to finally be joining in. Like I've been invited to some secret club, or a sect or cult. The trolley pushes itself through the store, filling with things I never imagined I'd buy, things I never thought I would want to buy. When there's no more room I heave the trolley through to the till, pay up, and lug the bags home, some gripped up under my arms, others hanging from my good wrist. The walk back is a struggle, but it's quick. I dump the bags just inside the front door and turn on my heels for round two. I head towards a different department store and load up the second trolley. All manner of things get thrown in: cleaning products, bedding sets, candles, a clock, plates, cups, standard, friendly looking ornaments and framed motivational posters. Signs that indicate what you're meant to do in each room, like *soak* and *relax*. I gather anything and everything that I feel would convince someone that I take pride in my home—that my home is an extension of my personality, of my tastes and likes. I briefly consider running off with the trolley as the bags are far too heavy to manage with one good hand and a growing sense of fatigue, but I can't be that person with a shopping trolley in their front garden. That's simply not the kind of establishment I'm aiming for. The second lot of shopping slows my walk home drastically. The bags swing in all directions and bash into the sides of my legs. The bruising on my hand starts to throb as the last of the painkillers wears off, and the plastic handles of the carrier bags burrow into my skin.

I decorate how I imagine she would decorate: girly but adult, feminine but with a slight hint of professionalism. I roll my newly purchased rug out on the living room floor, brushing out the creases to hide the stained carpet underneath. The new lampshades are more complicated to fit than I had imagined and send a cascade of choking dust down onto the floor. The main light fixture in the living room only has two working bulbs left—the other three fixtures have been holding dead bulbs for months. After some encouragement, the old bulbs loosen enough for me to change them, throwing fresh, bright light over the room for the first time. I scrub the kitchen again, dowsing it in another layer of bleach, and fill the cupboards with matching plates, mugs, crockery, bowls, and cooking utensils. I dot candles throughout the flat, lighting a few as I go to dissipate the musty smell of dust lifting off the old carpet. For the first time in months, I make the bed. It's therapeutic, really, shaking the new duvet out of its tight roll of plastic, freeing it from its thin, synthetic skin. Fighting the fitted bed sheet over the mattress, forcing the corners to stay down simultaneously. I bought a matching throw and cushions, more candles and annoying predictable models of the Buddha and ornaments of butterflies. Things I assume she likes. Things I now like. I sit on the edge of the bed for a few minutes, staring out into the hallway, scrunching my toes up in the fluff of the new rug that lines the bottom of the bed.

The bathroom takes more time and careful planning. Every inch of the room needs scrubbing with bleach until it shines and the grouting no longer outlines the tiles with a thick line of grime. The new bath mat sits perfectly on the floor and instantly brightens the room. I run my fingers through the bobbles and fold out the matching towels in the same shade of mauve. I line up the soap dish and toothbrush holder, shifting them, so they are an even distance away from the now sparkling tap. I grab the bag sat on the end of the bed containing everything new that I bought for the bathroom. I empty it slowly onto the side: one extra toothbrush in a dark shade of blue, men's shampoo and shower gel, a comb, some hair wax, and an electric shaver. They lay in line on the gleaming white surface by the sink, perfectly aligned and straight, stood to attention. I bought them all for him. He'll need them when he moves in.

The ritual continues much the same way in the bedroom. I thought it would be nice to buy him some of those expensive white shirts that he always wears. I iron them first, of course, pressing the creases therapeutically from the clean white fabric, and slide them into his side of the wardrobe. I don't know if he wears pyjamas, but I imagine not. I imagine him to sleep in just his boxers and maybe an old tee shirt. Or maybe I'd be in one of his old tee shirts, like in the films, the shirt barely covering my upper legs, skimming seductively against my underwear. I sit on the bed and picture it. Us waking up in the warm summer months, rolling out of the covers and letting the sun fall gently across our faces. Not long now.

It's like I'm laying things out for a newborn baby, organising them and sorting them, preparing their home for their arrival. Making sure everything is just so. Or perhaps it's more like preparing a body for burial. Laying out their Sunday best, preparing the flat like a tomb or a crypt to transport them to the afterlife; to preserve them and their memory forevermore. Either way, there are striking similarities.

I pace my way through my pop-up home for a while, bracing myself for the final room. It sucks the life out of me, standing there, staring at it from the doorway. Draws all of my energy from my mouth and nostrils and sends it gushing out of the tiny window. It's so much bigger than I remember and so much more hollow. I begin unpacking a few decorative items that I would never have bothered with before, rolling them from their newspaper wrappings. I scrub the fireplace, the sponge coming away greyer than the carpet but revealing the polished bricks that I'd almost entirely forgotten survived under the dust and dirt. Scented candles now perch on either end, symmetrical, in height order. I managed to find a small, flat pack bookshelf during my second visit to town, and I struggle with the instructions until it is successfully in one piece. I order the second-hand fiction books alphabetically and by genre, and I place the most interesting looking one on top of the shelf to make it look like I've been reading it. Next, I take out the photo frames, unwrap them carefully and polish the glass fronts. I don't actually have any photographs to home in the frames, but I don't think this is a problem. Liam doesn't need to know about my strained family life, so I leave the pre-printed images and happy, euphoric stock photo families in the frames where they are. They look perfect. Every image is different but with the same people. I can easily pass them off as my family.

'Oh, this is just my brother and sister-in-law visiting Niagara Falls. I'd love to go someday,' I practice aloud. 'Oh, you've never been? I'm sure we can go together. I promise not to push you in.'
I pad across to another frame, laughing to myself.

'This one was my first dog, Scamp. We used to walk him along the lakes. Beautiful old soul he was.'

Liam will fall for it. How could he not? They're my perfect, stock photo family. It's like I've flicked through the Argos catalogue and circled the ones I want. A family just to look good, one that could never argue or shun you or outcast you.

'Oh, I love my family. I'm so lucky to have such an amazing family, but they all just live so far away. It gets tricky, but we talk all the time.' Practice makes perfect, as they say.

I place my imprisoned family, held captive in their cheap, wooden frames and protected by their glass barriers, around the room. Suffocating in their makeshift cells. Family that can't talk back, can't have any impact on my life or the decisions I make, can't manipulate me and torture me and play with my emotions. I like them like this, suspended in reality and silenced by their fiction; my perfect little petri dish family.

Just a few finishing touches and we're ready; a few more subtle lies to weave together to make the whole thing convincing. I line up a shoe rack in the hall, perfectly straight against the far wall amongst the ghosts of the takeaway leaflets. It's slightly humorous, given I only own two pairs of shoes and one pair of beach flip flops that I'll never have a cause to wear. The shoes slide into place, symmetrical and evenly spaced apart, leaving enough room for the slippers I picked up for him earlier. I don't want him getting cold or uncomfortable. They sit on the end of the rack; it's only fair that they should have their own space. He'll be living here after all. Mine, right next to his. It'll only be a matter of time until all the parts of our lives are plaited together, tied neatly at the end. I've made sure he has his own mug, his own dressing gown, his own clothes, his own comb, and toothbrush. I've thought of everything to make moving in as comfortable as possible for him. He still needs a level of independence, after all. I don't want to become the overbearing girlfriend, but I can't wait for him to understand how much I depend on him to breathe, to live, to exist.

I brush the carpet out in the hall, laying the bristles all the same way and lifting the dust into the air. The small cupboard by the door stands slightly open, it's uneven, almost triangular shaped door ajar. I shove it with my foot, tucking the length of thick rope back inside, knocking something solid with my toes. I bend down to close the door properly, the hallway light catching the metal of the handcuffs left over from the last time. I like to think none of this stuff will be at all necessary, but I'd rather have it there just in case. Just a few supplies, sort of an insurance policy I suppose.

Everything looks perfect, like I tore my new home straight from the pages of a magazine–Woman's Weekly perhaps. He's going to love it, I know he will.

I make my way to my new bedroom, plush and clean and welcoming. It's the first thing I lay eyes on, hanging over the door of the wardrobe, on *my* side of the bed. The last thing I need to find a home for. I don't know for sure when I'll find a use for it, but it's encouraging having it there as another option.

I stand in front of it and watch it for a few moments, as if it's got the ability to get up and move, maybe greet me as I walk in. I watch it–hanging from the top of the wardrobe, the bag like a heavy shadow against the pale wood of the sliding door. The zip slips down the length of the bag, unveiling a deep flash of red fabric, the bag splitting open like a deep, bloody gauge against dark flesh. I pull it out of the dress bag, removing the heart from the cavity I've torn, and I lay it ceremoniously on the bed. The edges need pushing out, flattening the red print of a body onto the duvet. I've never owned anything like it before. It's beautiful. A sleek and stunning knee-length dress in the deepest shade of blood red. The sleeves hang seductively off the shoulders, dripping red fabric down the length of the arm, pooling just above the wrists.

Red is such a powerful, seductive colour. It clings to my frame, my hips and shoulders, staring back at me from the mirror, shocking red against my porcelain skin. The blue of my eyes deepens in contrast to the bright fabric. I love it. He'll love it. I hold it for a few more seconds, imagining what it will be like to have the smooth fabric pressed against my skin, clinging to my hips and skimming over my navel, imagining what it will be like to finally have him living here with me—how amazing every second will be. I indulge my fantasies for a few more seconds before sliding the dress back into the bag, concealing the blood red silk in the black plastic before slipping it between the other clothes in my wardrobe. Hiding it in plain sight.

I slip out of my jeans and old, worn jumper, letting them slide into a pile on the floor and exchange them for new pyjamas—matching of course. I sit on the divan, swinging my legs in and pull back the covers on my freshly made bed. I wonder if I'll sleep better in a bed, rather than scrunched up in an armchair? I climb in, letting my head sink into the feather pillows enclosed in their silk cases, pulling the duvet right up under my chin. The softness of the quilt and the pillows wrap around my skin, swallowing me and pulling me beneath consciousness. I think I will. My eyes sink into my skull, my tongue relaxes and falls away from the roof of my mouth, and I wait, as my body lifts and falls into a sudden and deep sleep.

Chapter Seven

There are a few more things left to arrange ready for Liam's arrival, but there's no rush—we've got all the time in the world. I just need to get some groceries that don't require microwaving and potentially some fruit and vegetables, so he thinks that I'm conscious of being healthy. Of course I'm not, but he would rather I am, so from now on, I am health-aware. I am in control of my own body, I am mindful. Maybe I'll take up yoga. I need to practice being tidier too. I can tell he's painfully organised, so therefore, I am now obsessed with being organised.

I spotted the perfect armchair for Liam yesterday; the perfect accompaniment to my own in one of the department stores. It was there, in the corner, probably an out of season number or one left over from a set that someone else bought. I'd have grabbed it there and then, but there was no way I'd have been able to get it home. I need to go back and get it today.

There are less people on the streets today, less people to get in my way. I walk quickly into town, my head hanging down to the floor watching the pavement fall away under my feet.

I go back to the department store. The lights are glaringly bright and white, cutting in comparison to the cloudy sky. There are more people here than I imagined there would be.

They're cluttering around rails of clothing, clustering in queues and swarming towards changing rooms. It's warm. I push my way through the growing crowds towards the furniture in the corner, hoping that some other customer hasn't snapped up the chair. It's still there, and it's perfect. The heavy fabric is a rich navy blue—his colour—and flocked velvet. It's luxurious and a hint extravagant, but just understated enough not to be too imposing. It's masculine and strong, and will look even better with him sitting in it. I jot down the order number and stumble my way back through the hoards towards the till. The queue stands, imposing and long, snaking through the aisles. One deep breath in to steady myself and I join the end, watching those in front of me and letting my mind wander as I wait.

There is a boy in the queue in front of me. He doesn't mean any harm; I don't think. His hands are all over the place, picking at things on his Mum's jacket, pulling on the trolley and whining.

'I want to go home.'

I know you do kid, so do I. Trust me.

He's relentless. Still tugging on the hem of his Mum's coat, moaning and whimpering like an injured animal. His hands are at his face, picking at his hair, tugging on the metal of the trolley.

Pathetic. I want him to shut up. Why won't he shut up?

My hands inch their way closer to him until they're centimetres away from his pale, pink throat. Just a few inches more and I could make him be quiet; I could do him a favour and make him give up his complaining. Hot breath floods out of my nostrils over my top lip. I could do everyone here a favour. My fingers are almost touching him now; and even so, he's still moaning. They're wrapping around his tiny neck—I could do this with one hand, he's so small. And somehow, despite what's going on, he's still grumbling. His skinny throat is warm on my palm, and I clench, tight and strong and—

'Next customer, please.'

Visions of his tiny face flash across my eyes. The blood, the life flickering in his irises like a failing light bulb.

'Excuse me? Next customer, please.'

'Oh, god, sorry,' I say, handing over the product number on the scrap of paper. My hands tremble as the cashier manages to pry the paper from my fingers.

'Delivery?' The voice is monotone, uninterested.

'Erm, yes, sorry,' I fluster, panicked, like I've been caught stealing. 'As soon as possible.'

'Tomorrow morning, 7 a.m.?' Her eyes don't leave the computer screen and a small, blue biro bobs up and down in the corner of her mouth.

'Yes, yes that's fine.' My hand automatically thrusts a wad of cash in her face, anything to speed this up and get me out of this shop quicker. I virtually sprint out onto the pavement, the kid's groans still vaguely recognisable behind me. He's still grovelling to his Mum. She's not paying any attention to him, so I doubt he'll stop any time soon.

His tiny face follows me the whole way home, through the supermarket, sheltering and hiding between tins and boxes of food. It doesn't scare me, though. I find it comforting; to know how much power I could have had over such a small life. I could control that light behind his eyes–he's still breathing because of a choice I just made. I'm riding high on the power that his weakness has fed deep in my chest. Despite literally feeling his soft skin under my fingertips, despite sensing his vocal chords and veins cramp under the pressure I could have inflicted, he's still alive.

I sit for a while in a new coffee shop, a different spot, a deliberate step away from the usual café. This could be our new spot–one not tainted by memories of her and the bitter taste of betrayal. The views are nicer here. I take a seat by the window, facing out towards a water fountain surrounded by dainty wooden benches. The water tumbles from the hoses, pattering and spraying on the glassy surface and chucking a light spray into the humid air. There are children–just a few, maybe 4 or 5 years old. Their fingers ripple through the water. They fling loose coins into the pool, the pennies hitting the surface and the water swallowing the children's wishes whole. You can see it in their faces if you look hard enough. They believe in their wishes and magic and miracles. You can hear it in their laughter, tainted with innocence. One day Liam and I will hear that laughter, one day we'll have our own little miracle. Another mouth to feed, a life to put before your own and realise that your life no longer centres around you – you're no longer the main character.

I know how I'd raise a child–oh so differently from the way my mother tried to raise me. I hardly remember what she looks like; I haven't seen her in so long. Sometimes I try to force myself to see her, just in my imagination. I remember the obvious things, the things that don't affect her personality or let me see anything past the surface. Her limp, dark hair hanging in strands over her face, clinging to the sweat on the back of her neck. Her dark, unfeeling eyes. Those, I remember. But her personality and her voice? Those I've forced myself to forget. It's startling, seeing her face, even as a figment of my imagination. She's the reason I'm living out here, alone, away from anyone else I know or have ever cared about. She forced me out here, and I chose to stay. My head rests heavily against my hand as I look out at the children as they play. There's a small girl in a pretty pink outfit sitting by the fountain and playing with a doll. They seem so blissfully unaware at that age, so happy at the smallest, most trivial things. She looks a bit like mine, from back home. Dark hair, shocking blue eyes. My first great love, before Liam. The reason I'm living out here, away from my family, away from my friends, away from my hometown. Such a beautiful little girl.

I finish the coffee and walk home, bags in tow. I haven't worked out exactly what day Liam will move in, but it will be soon, I can feel it. Everything around me seems brighter and more vivid at the thought of having him in my home, like someone's turned up the saturation, whacked up the colour. Soon it will be our home.

I wish the rest of the day away. I've got nothing left to do except reshuffle things in the flat, things that I've already rearranged a hundred times or more. I put out a few more photographs, balancing the stock images snug in their frames behind the cool glass. With each photo, I imagine what it would be like to be related to these people, these picture perfect, symmetrical, aesthetically pleasing people, almost impossible people. This one, the one stood under the silver birch tree–she could be my sister. For Liam, I will call her Jenny. I've always fancied myself as a Jenny, but I'm a Sarah, so this lady, my sister, is now Jenny. Jenny is in two photos– the one under the tree and the one with a young, fair-haired man stood by what I assume is Niagara Falls. There's a beautiful image of an older lady sat in a rocking chair on the patio of a small house in the countryside. I will now refer to this lady as my grandmother. My grandmother–caring, warm, smells like freshly baked bread–all the stereotypical, usual things I would expect from a grandmother. Of course, my grandmother was nothing like that. She was crass and harsh, hit my brother and me for speaking out of turn, hated my personality and couldn't accept me for who I was. She was the spitting image of her daughter–my mother—who I would rather pretend was dead than admit was alive and well and had chosen not to talk to me for the last decade or so. She's chosen to believe I was dead, so I wish her the same fate. Together they disagreed with every ounce of my personality. I'll show them that I can be happy and have a successful life without them. The last picture is on the windowsill. It is of an older gentleman and what I'd presume is his granddaughter. They both have dark hair and tanned complexions and warm, inviting brown eyes. The man looks gentle and kind, with strong worn hands and a face that has a serious story to tell. For Liam, they are now my father and perhaps a niece, or something similar. I've formed the perfect stock-photo family. They're much easier to deal with than my own.

I shuffle some candles around on the mantelpiece. A few small ornaments perch on the edge, the kind that you receive from an Aunt or Uncle at Christmas, that you don't really want but you have to display to look grateful.

Everything looks and feels perfect. It's welcoming and warm and ready to house a happy couple starting a family. After I've decided that nothing else needs rearranging, I go through the usual ritual before bed. I think this is it; I feel quite certain of it, actually. This will be the last night I eat alone. The last night I sleep alone. Tomorrow, Liam will move in, and we will begin our lives together.

This is the last time I will fall asleep with only the sound of my own heartbeat.

Chapter Eight

I dream of his face, of his eyes, his nose, his lips. I think about kissing those lips and resting my head on his shoulder as we sleep in our bed together for the first time. Breathing in his warm scent, being wrapped up by his warmth and finally feeling safe. It's getting closer, I can feel it, pulling at the corners of my heart like tiny chords tying me to him. I dream of running my fingers over his cool, granite skin, smooth and cold under my fingertips. Placing my lips on his motionless, icy mouth. Placing my hands and my head on his still chest, listening out for the heartbeat that never comes.

A shrill buzzing pierces the silence as my eyes fly open against the heavy darkness. I stumble around on the floor, scraping together the clothes I wore yesterday, forcing them over my head and dragging them down my face. A chain, a sliding bolt and a normal keyhole lock the door, and they all stiffen the second they sense I'm in a rush. I fling the small copper disc away from the wide-angle peephole to reveal a large man clad in a bright red uniform—the man from the department store. The door swings inwards, revealing the protruding clipboard and pen hanging from a tattered piece of string.

'Morning. Armchair yours?'

I nod, grab the pen and scrawl my illegible signature across the bottom of the A4 piece of paper. The man tucks the board under his arm silently and waddles up the path to retrieve the armchair. He wheels the chair back down the path, twisting it awkwardly through the front door and laying it to rest in front of the living room. He places his hand on the door to the living room, threatening to open it.

'Oh, no it's fine, thank you. I can move it from here.'

He looks me up and down, scrutinising my small frame and injured hand but quickly relents.

'Alright.' He shrugs and leaves without another word.

I didn't want the door open; I'm happy to struggle moving it later. I didn't want him to see in, to invade my privacy.

The chair stands defiantly, blocking up the narrow hallway at the landing of my flat. It clogs up the thoroughfare; a massive lump stuck in my throat. The chair is perfect; Liam is perfect. But what if Liam doesn't fit in, just as the chair doesn't? What if, no matter how hard I try, he still protrudes and juts out and refuses to blend in with the rest of my life? I'm happy to welcome him, but will he be happy to be welcomed?

I lean over the top of the chair and flick the handle to the living room, watching the door slide inwards. The chair shunts across the carpet into the living room as I heave it across the floor and eventually slide it next to my own. I envisage us sitting there together, growing old gracefully next to each other. Our two armchairs surrounded by bookshelves, linked together by the rug on the floor. Children playing at our feet, cups of warm tea nestled in between our hands as we read late into the evening.

It's easy to lose yourself in the idea of making memories. I steal a quick glance at my watch. The morning's hours have slipped through my fingers. Despite being up in plenty of time, I'll need to rush if I want to get into the office on time. I fumble into the bathroom, re-wrapping my hand in a fresh bandage, concealing the deep purple bruising as best I can. I'll be lucky if I meet Liam this morning what with the delay the chair has caused me. I curse my lack of organisation and timekeeping and make a mental note to get better. Liam is incredibly organised, and he'd hate for me to be consistently late or messy or disorganised. I'd change, for him. I will change, if I have to. The only constant is change.

I leave the flat at a semi-jog, pulling my coat over my shoulders as I leave and curse my lateness. Liam is nowhere to be seen. I must have missed him this morning. My lips purse and I scold myself under my breath. I'll see him later on at the coffee shop anyway, but I'd built myself up to see his face. I'd been looking forward to seeing him this morning, a fresh image to place in the armchair for whilst I'm at work. I rush into the office, bursting through the door with minutes to spare. My face is warm from running up the stairs, and I can feel the eyes of the office on me. The silence is nothing but awkward.

'Morning,' I say in between breaths to break the silence. No one responds. They don't even look up from their desks or make eye contact. They just continue to work or talk to each other and ignore my arrival entirely. It's as if I never uttered a word.

I stride to my office, dump my bags on the floor by my desk and head straight to the kitchen for the morning's first coffee. No one reacts to my arrival. The silence is palpable. Ellis is in there, as usual, making herself and a handful of others their first morning beverage.

She sees me and makes full eye contact, but still doesn't say anything. She looks over her shoulder, straight through me and continues to fumble with the teaspoons and coffee grains. I don't know what I've done to annoy everyone this morning, but I've clearly done something to warrant this kind of reaction.

'Morning, Ellis—everything okay?' I ask her hesitantly, confused by the atmosphere. Our conversation has returned to the robotic, stunted flow of the Monday morning. She doesn't react or return my greeting and continues to focus on the coffee cups in front of her, stirring deliberately and loudly. I can't work out what I've done. What did I do to irritate her? I walk around her grabbing a cup from the cupboard above her head.

She swings her body round to face me, staring straight at my hand. In my rush to leave the flat this morning, I failed to dress it properly. The beige bandage has slipped away from my hand and wrist, hanging limply in a loose 'u' shape just above my shirtsleeve. The mauve spatters and deep, dark billowing blue clouds glow proudly. I struggle to hide it, yanking my sleeve over my wrist, but she's already seen it.

'My god, Sarah–what happened to you?' She recoils, her voice a mixture of genuine concern and unmistakeable disgust. 'What happened to your hand?'

'Oh, this? I--I just had an accident,' I say, pulling my hand away from the shelf by her face and holding it towards my chest. 'I fell. I was buying some new things for the flat, and I fell carrying boxes in the hallway. Silly, really. It looks a lot worse than it is. I bruise very easily.' I hold it up to her, trying to move it without wincing to convince her that it does indeed look worse than it is. The bandage has fully slipped away, draping across my forearm. I thought my lie was convincing enough, but Ellis's face says otherwise. I frankly couldn't care less if she believes me or not. She doesn't need to know the truth. No one but me will ever know the truth.

'It looks bad, Sarah. Did you do it on Saturday? Is that why you didn't make it to my place?'

It takes a second or two to dawn on me - our conversation on Friday seemed so long ago. It felt as though weeks had passed since I'd agreed to meet her socially, outside of work. I'd forgotten all about Ellis's invite. I have a sudden rush of guilt, which is quickly replaced by a deep sense of relief. I didn't really want to go anyway and the 'accident,' as we'll hereby call it, has given me a very viable 'out.' I quickly shift my facial expression from confused to apologetic.

'Oh God, Ellis, I'm so sorry. I did do it Saturday afternoon, and after spending a few hours in the walk-in centre I completely forgot about our plans. I'm so sorry.' I could go on grovelling like this for hours. It's so easy to play into her hands, and I can see pity cross her face already. She feels sorry for me. She believes me. It's like taking candy from a baby.

'No, don't be silly, there's no need to apologise. Are you sure it's okay, Sarah? It really doesn't look too healthy.' Ellis leans forward in an attempt to get a closer look again, and I pull my hand up to my chest to guard it from her prying eyes.

'Oh, honestly it's fine,' I say, forcing a small smile on my face. 'Anyway, work calls. I'll catch you later.' I grab my mug and stride out of the kitchen, coffee swilling and sloshing over the edge of the cup and onto my uninjured hand. Her eyes are on my back as I walk away. She did seem genuinely concerned, but I've got too much to plan today to waste anymore time loitering in the kitchen.

I need to work out the perfect way to ask Liam to move in with me, to get him through the front door and to convince him that I'm the one he needs. Once he's in, I've got no doubt that he'll stay, but the real challenge will be getting him through the front door.

My fingers tap across the raised keys of my computer, feigning interest in my job. I'm meant to be working, but realistically I'm wracking my brain trying to think of the best way to do this. Is it best to lie to get him through the front door and then worry about the rest afterwards? He'd understand if I lied to him, I think. I'd be lying for love and for our sakes after all. Or perhaps I should just trust that he loves me the way I love him and ask him to move in? But that leaves the option of him saying no. And I've worked far too hard for him to simply not want to move in with me. That would be far too risky. I sit and think for what feels like hours, nervously raking my nails across the palms of my hands until they're red and raw, chewing the tip of my biro anxiously. I can't think here. I think I'll be better off in the flat, waiting for the inspiration to hit me.

Chapter Nine

Liam.

I go to the same place for coffee every day. Not because their coffee is particularly good or the surroundings are exceedingly brilliant. It's mostly because I'm lazy. If I've found something I like that works for me, then I won't change it unless I absolutely have to. Unless something changes or forces me to make a change. The coffee here is fine, the staff are friendly enough and don't expect me to tip every time I visit, and there is always a good selection of newspapers to rifle through.

I do enjoy the routine of it all. I like arriving at around the same time every day and ordering the same coffee every day and flicking to the back of the newspaper to get to the sports pages every day. The rest of my life seems so unpredictable and unbearably busy that sitting in the same coffee shop every day for half an hour grounds me and reminds me that I am in fact in control of at least some small, insignificant element of my day-to-day.

Today is like every other day. I enjoy its predictability. It is unremarkable in every sense of the word, and that's absolutely fine. Today could be any Monday in my past or perhaps any Monday in my future. I sit in my usual spot, grab the newspaper and relax for the precious 30 minutes of freedom I have from my increasingly grey, corporate job.

I know this coffee shop like the back of my hand now. I know every regular face, every employee, every option and odd, previously unheard of flavour of coffee. And I also know that someone is missing. There are a handful of us that come in here at the same time every day and sit in the same seats every day. We all leave our various jobs from various corners of the town and seem to meet here. Not to ever talk to each other, but to share in the space at the coffee shop. To change the order would be unthinkable. I usually sit on the second table closest to the till, in the middle of all the action and with a good viewpoint for the other customers for a spot of people watching. There's an older gentleman in a plaid farmer's hat who sits to my left. He always has a pot of tea and brings a novel. He's here when I arrive and is still sitting there reading when I walk out. For all I know, he may never actually leave. There's the older lady, as well, that sits directly in front of me, at the table with the squishy, sofa-like armchairs. She normally has a magazine and drinks any weird and wonderful caffeinated concoction that the baristas can dream up for her. Some sugary, syrup filled drink, no doubt. Then there's the other lady. The mysterious dark-eyed, raven-haired young woman who sits in the window to my left. She has a latte, sometimes cake on a good day. She might be reading or browsing on her phone, but no matter what she is doing, she always looks like she is away with the fairies. She always looks so sickeningly happy that I often wish I were inside her head. I wish I knew what she was thinking. She's always alone, which I found odd at first, but then realised I was usually on my own as well, except when Jennifer insists on escorting me to the coffee shop, as if I'm going to get lost between here and the office. I like Jennifer, don't get me wrong. But she can be suffocating. She wants something far more serious than I'm willing or able to give. I usually slip away from the office before she notices. Maybe she thinks I'm a flight risk. Maybe I am. I have quite loudly expressed that I might just leg it one day. Move to the country, change career, go back to university–who knows what the plan would be? Who cares, to be honest. Just any kind of change would be good now. Any escape from this tedium.

I go back to reading. I stare at the crossword for a while, but the answers don't strike me, so I give up pretty quickly. I stir a hard cube of sugar into my coffee, watching it lose its form and dissolve into the brown liquid. I look up as she piles through the door in a hurry, the bell ringing frantically on her entry and the door swinging behind her. Her raven-black hair is scraped away from her face, piled on top of her head. Dark strands have stuck in wisps around her forehead, clinging to her sweaty skin. I've never seen her like this before: distressed, worried, anxious. She goes to order her coffee–skimmed milk latte–and takes her usual seat. I continue to watch her over the top of the newspaper I'm pretending to read. She looks really shaken up. I watch as she fumbles in her bag and pulls out her phone, which seems to be ringing non-stop. She answers and whispers into the handset, cupping her face in her hand to conceal what she is saying. I can't quite make out her words, but she looks a mess. Her eyes are startled and bloodshot, black smudges of makeup swept across her face and under her eyelids. Her face is puffy and exhausted, grey from a lack of sleep and too much caffeine. I continue to drink my coffee and desperately strain my ears to try to hear what she is saying. She looks like she might be in trouble, or perhaps she's not very well, or she's received some really terrible news.

Just as I'm pondering what it could possibly be that has got her in this state, her hand flashes into my vision. I don't know what she has done to it, but it looks horrific. It's swollen and speckled with puddles of multiple shades of deep purple and mottled green. The skin is stretched so tightly over the flesh that it looks like it could split or burst at any moment, like sausage meat escaping its thin casing. It looks bad, but she's clearly not been to a doctor or the hospital. There's a bandage, loosely hanging around her hand.

I manage to catch a few words that seep through the speaker of her mobile. It sounds like she's talking to someone about her boyfriend - her mother, maybe? She's whispering, but she's hysterical. A few words escape; I can see her mouthing them. Her boyfriend hurt her. He swung for her or threw something at her, I'm not sure. So she tried to hit him, but he was too quick and moved out of her way, pushing her over and into the wall. That would explain the hand, which clearly needs medical attention. She's crying, I think. Or if she isn't, then she certainly has been.

God, how horrific. I don't know this woman at all, but I feel like I should help her, comfort her, do something to alleviate some of the pain she is feeling. I know I'm staring, but I can't make myself stop. There's something so captivating about this woman, her tears, her pain, it's almost as if she wants me to look. I've finished my coffee, but I wait around until she's finished hers, just to see if she says anything else to the person at the other end of the phone. She holds her head in her hands, the phone still pressed to her ear, listening to the person at the other end of the line. She doesn't utter another word; she just continues to cry to herself.

I watch from behind my newspaper as she finishes her latte, hangs up the phone and dabs her eyes with a well-used tissue that she's pulled from her pocket. She is distraught and exhausted; her face blotched with patches of red and pink.

A few deep breaths later she gathers herself, grabbing her belongings and fumbling out of the café onto the street. I decide to follow her. I don't know why, exactly, but my body has made the decision for me, and I don't argue. My feet carry me out of the coffee shop before I give my mind a chance to convince me otherwise.

I'm not really following her, not in that way. I just need to see she's okay. She turns left where I would usually turn right, but I still follow, just a few feet behind. I grope around in my pocket for my phone in an effort to look inconspicuous.

She only makes it a few steps before collapsing in a heap onto the nearest bench. She's crying, gasping for air and weeping, her torso shuddering with every sob. I don't know what to do. I should probably just turn away and walk back to work, leave her alone, not invade her privacy. I don't even know the woman, but I feel so inclined to help her. I know I should leave, I know it would be best to turn around and no one would be any the wiser. But I can't bring myself to do it.

I sit down beside her. I want to help her, but I don't know how. I try not to look directly at her and realise almost immediately that this was a mistake; I need to leave. I get up from the bench, my face feeling hot with embarrassment, but she's seen me already.

'What do you want?' She spits the words at me across the bench. She looks up at me with almost entirely black eyes brimming with tears.

'Sorry, I—I'm sorry, I just saw that you were upset.' I can hardly string a sentence together. 'I wanted to make sure you were okay.' God, it sounds ridiculous when I say it out loud. *Hello madam, yes I'm very aware that I don't have a clue who you are or what's happened to you. I was just wondering if you'd trust a complete stranger to help you.* Brilliant. I can see that she clearly is not okay, far from it actually, but I can't think of what else would be appropriate to say. I should not still be sitting here. I'm just making things worse. I should just leave at speed.

She shifts her body away from me.

'"You don't even know me, get away from me!' She looks like she might be about to stand up, but she doesn't move. Her eyes lock onto mine, her face a mixture of fury, pain and confusion. The anger has seeped into the corners of her face turning her expression rigid and steely, but I can see beneath that–I can see that she's found herself in a really bad situation. I honestly don't know what's come over me, but I've let it lead me into this scenario, and I don't know what to do to, realistically, get me out of it, so I keep pushing.

'Is everything okay?' I ask again, stammering. 'Do you need me to call someone for you? Has something happened?'

I can see that she doesn't really want to answer any of those questions. She stares at me for a moment longer, the harsh anger lifting from her cheekbones to be replaced by confusion at my desperation to help her. She's crying again, sobbing with renewed energy. The tears flood down her cheeks, and she throws her head against my chest, wailing and crying. I jerk back at first, my back slamming into the metal of the bench sending a jolt of pain flying up my spine. I don't know what I expected her to do, but it wasn't this. She cries without breathing for minutes at a time, her tears soaking my shirt and smears of dark makeup smudging onto my collar. This was a mistake. I should have left her, but I can hardly walk away now.

Eventually, she comes up for air. Fresh tears have drawn tracks across her swollen pink cheeks. She looks utterly broken.

I--,' she poises herself to talk but reconsiders. 'I don't really know that I should tell you. It's not really appropriate.' She wipes her hand across her face, dragging black mascara around her eyes and cheeks. I hand her a tissue and give her time to catch her breath again before talking. Her speech is broken, perforated with short gasps and whimpers.

She takes a deep breath. 'It's my boyfriend. He--he hurt me.' The last few words tumble from her lips, as if they've been pent up inside her for some time and were desperate to be freed. As if the truth of the whole situation has been locked away behind her clenched teeth, hidden behind botched foundation and unravelling bandages. She looks up at me with eyes filled with unimaginable pain and flings her head back into my shoulder, returning to the intense sobs and shudders of the few minutes prior. Her hands are shaking in her lap, her delicate fingers trembling as she sobs.

'Calm down--just breathe,' I say, placing my hands on her shoulders and encouraging her to sit upright to catch her breath. *What have I got myself into?* 'Do you need me to call someone for you? Do you need to go to the police? I can come with you if you like.' *God, please say no.*

She shakes her head. She is wholly defeated, beaten into submission. It's terrible to witness someone so fragile and helpless, overcome with emotion and nerves. I feel like I've opened the door on a very private scene and I'm staring in at something I ought not to be witnessing. She starts to slow her breathing, forcing her shoulders to drop and her posture to relax against the back of the hard bench. She looks to be calming down, at least for the time being. Her eyes are fixated on the grey concrete between her feet, anchoring her concentration.

'What's your name?' I'm not sure what makes me break the silence–I just know I can't stomach the quiet for much longer. I think if I know her name she might open up to me. Maybe she'll feel that she can speak to me, let me know what she needs or what I can do to make this better. It's completely illogical, but this whole situation is very much warped in my mind.

She's wrestling with her conscience; I can see it in her face. Why would she open up to a stranger like me, when she's clearly been so hurt by someone she loves? She sits for a few minutes longer, playing with the tips of her fingers and tugging at a loose thread from her shirtsleeve.

'Sarah,' she croaks against her dry throat. 'It's Sarah.'

'Sarah,' I confirm aloud, nodding encouragingly. 'Is there anything I can do to help you, Sarah?' I've slipped into work-mode. I sound professional and hard, despite trying my best not to.

'No, I don't think there is,' she replies, pulling at the tissue in her lap and leaving shards of damp white paper across her thighs. The tears are slipping in silence down her cheeks now, tumbling off her chin and onto her jumper. The sobbing has stopped, the shudders and gasps for air have lifted off her shoulders, but the tears continue. I can't leave her like this.

'Do you want me to walk with you for a bit. Will that help at all?'

She wipes her face with the remains of the scrunched up tissue and nods. She still looks terrified but seems to be regaining control of her emotions. We pace around the fountain in the middle of the high street; walking quietly side-by-side, listening to the world and watching the people go by. The noises are muffled and muted as if we're walking around surrounded by a bubble or glass wall. Her hands are buried deep in the pockets of her coat, and her shoulders are hunched, curling protectively around her torso. I watch my feet as they hit the pavement, occasionally glancing up to check that she's still there, that she hasn't bolted away from me. I've shoved my hands deep in my pockets, pulling on a tiny loose thread to ease my nerves. This woman, Sarah, is so small and so delicate, and has been violated and abused by someone who is meant to love her more than anyone else in the world. Someone she trusts, someone she opened her world up to and let walk right in, has destroyed her. I'm sad and nauseated to think that her trust has been violated and ruined in that way; a beautiful, sad woman completely devastated by one horrific experience.

'He, sorry, my boyfriend, came home late last night. He was drunk and angry. I think maybe he'd been gambling or something; he was really livid. I tried to console him when he came in, but he wanted none of it. He got angrier the more I tried to help him. I was just trying to help him; all I ever want to do is help him.' The tears are falling again, soundlessly. Her voice is barely more than a squeak, a high-pitched, broken whisper. 'I tried to help him, maybe more than he deserved. I tried but he–he hit me, a few times. He shoved me about and went to push me. It wasn't the first time, and I'd just had enough, so I finally got the courage together to defend myself. I tried to hit him. I really wanted to hit him. I've dreamt of it, you know? Of finally gathering the courage and the strength, of swinging my arm back and the feeling of my knuckles slamming into his cheek and feeling the bone groan under my fist, but he moved. He moved out of the way and shoved me into the wall, and I fell.'

The tears are still brimming, but less so now. She wipes her nose on her sleeve, crossing her arms tightly across her chest and pursing her wet lips together. 'He laughed at me.' I could tell she hasn't told anyone this before; she is really struggling to come to terms with what he's done to her. 'It's not the first time, but it was definitely the worst. He comes home late, a lot. If I question where he's been, he lashes out. It's because he thinks I don't trust him, but I do. I really do. I love him. Even after all this, even after all the bullying and the shouting and hitting and the screaming. Even after imagining what it would feel like to finally connect with his skin and make him feel the pain he forces on me. I still love him. And I have no idea what to do.'

'God I'm...I'm so sorry.' I don't know how else to respond–what to say that would reassure her in any way.

'I'm going to leave him now. That's it. I can't do this anymore. I can't love just to be unloved and beaten in return. I really do want to leave him, but it's so much harder than just walking away, you know?'

I nod my understanding. I'm glad she intends to leave him. No one deserves to be treated that way, to have to live in constant fear that your partner might tip over the edge and take you down with them at any point. I can't bring myself to say anything to her, as much as I think she needs to hear some words of kindness.

She looks up at me again, tears glistening in pools in her eyes, threating to break the seal, but no longer sobbing. 'Sorry, you really didn't need to hear all of that on a Monday morning,' she says, the corners of her lips straining into the tiniest hint of a smile. 'But thank you for listening.'

I return her gesture. Not a wide, happy smile, but more of an acknowledgement that I'm more than happy to lend a listening ear. Though I fear that it looks a bit patronising, maybe pitying.

'No, it's fine. Is there really nothing I can do to help? Anyone you'd like to call?'

'No,' she replies. 'I'm just going to go back to my flat, clean myself up and move on. That's all I want. I just want to forget it and get on with my life.'

I nod again. It's all I can think of to do.

'Will you walk with me?'

'Of course,' I respond.

We walk a few minutes in silence. The awkwardness seems to have left for now. Her flat is almost immediately opposite my office, perhaps a 10 or 15-minute walk from my home just across the park. I'm more than happy to walk her, to know she gets home safely. It's the least I can do.

'Oh, I'm so sorry,' she says. 'I never asked your name.'

'Don't be silly–you've had so much on your mind. It's Noah.'

Chapter Ten

Noah. No-ah. Noah.

I say it in my head. Let it roll around on my tongue and imagine what it would sound like if I were to say it out loud. Not sure I like it, actually. I'd really pictured him as a Liam. I guess I'll get used to it. We've got all the time in the world to get used to each other, after all. Or maybe I'll just keep calling him Liam. Fooling him was a lot easier than I could ever have hoped for. He played right into my hands. I suppose I am getting quite good at lying after all.

He was in the coffee shop bang on time today. I hid out in the park, preparing myself for my acting debut. I got myself upset, did a quick lap around the park to look out of breath and red in the face, and threw myself through the door into the coffee shop. It was much easier than I could ever have hoped. He immediately looked around. He must have noticed that I was late. I grabbed the usual coffee and took my seat, stage left. I pretended to be on the phone, frantically talking to an imaginary someone at the other end of the line, sobbing and whispering. I made a real effort to slip a few key words in there, saying them just a little too loudly so he could pick up on them. And he picked up on them, all right. I could see him wincing as I spoke, flinching, as I deliberately held out my injured hand, unwrapped and purple, on the table in front of me. He'd finished his coffee minutes before me. It had passed 11:30, the usual time that he leaves, and yet he still sat there, intrigued by my mysterious phone call. I finished up and he followed me as I bundled myself out of the door. It was ironic really, considering how long I've been following him unnoticed and here he was, shadowing me and tiptoeing behind me, though doing a terrible job at being inconspicuous. I pretended not to see him at first, to let him think he was doing a good job hiding behind me. I acted shocked to find him sat next to me on the bench and even got defensive for a few seconds. I was defensive and uptight for just the right amount of time, and once I eventually told him what had happened, he was like putty in my hands. Easy as pie. He was lapping my lies up whole-heartedly. I'm quite grateful for the practice I was able to get lying to Ellis in the office. It's actually scary, how easy it all came to me–like a duck to water. Once he joined me on the bench, it all came quite naturally. The lies flooded from my lips. I had to reign it in a few times, actually. I even convinced myself at some points.

It honestly could not have been any easier.

He feels terribly sorry for poor old me. The delicate, innocent, abused young woman, so fragile and slight and in such need of saving. I can see the pity in his eyes; I can taste it when he talks. He feels sorry for me, wants to help me wherever possible, even if he's clearly not sure why. He wants to rescue me, to fix me. I absolutely love how weak he thinks I am. As if I'd ever let someone attack me! He has no idea. I'm not the one who needs saving.

I'll let him believe he's the stronger one for a while longer. He offers to walk me home, and it's like he's read my mind. Like he's walking straight into my arms. It's meant to be.

Honestly, my plan could not have gone any better.

We're walking now, trying to make awkward small talk about the weather and all things British. I throw in a token sniff and the sad 'victim' eyes I've practiced along the way, just to keep it all going. I don't want to lose momentum now. The walk isn't far, anyway. I can see my flat–the door is edging closer and closer, getting bigger in my vision.

It's really quite hard to keep the wounded face going. It's like I have to physically hold the emotionally damaged, distraught mask against my face, against the building excitement that's fizzing away underneath the first layer of my skin. I stifle a giggle at one point, successfully disguising it as a tiny, exasperated whimper. This is it. This is what I've been waiting for, what I've been preparing for, what I've been building up to. He's almost mine, and he has absolutely no idea. I've never had to try so hard not to smile. It's taken all of my self-control not to laugh in his face. My heart is thudding in my chest, reverberating in my throat and just below my ears. An excitable wave of nausea floods over me. My palms are sweaty. I'm nervous, but also the most excited I think I've ever been about anything. Adrenaline is coursing through my body, bubbling away in my veins. Soon, he'll see how much I love him, how much I care for him, how much I've always loved him. And I can't wait to tell him. I can't wait for him to see what I've done for him. I can't wait for him to love me back. I can't wait to tell him that this was all for him. This act, all of it, is because I love him.

We're at the door. I fumble for my keys, deliberately dropping them and scrabble to the floor to pick them up and gather myself. He's standing there, not knowing how to say goodbye or what to do next. I can't let him go now, not now we've got this close.

'Thank you,' I grin and place my hand gently on his arm. 'Thank you for walking me back. Do you want to maybe come in for a cup of tea? It's really the least I can do.'

I can see him hesitating, having conflicting internal thoughts. I assume he's got work or some other commitment that he's meant to be doing this afternoon. I watch for a few seconds as he mentally argues with himself.

'Or, I mean, I understand if you can't–if you've got work or something. I'm sure I'll be alright on my own.' I wipe my sleeve across my face and look down to the floor, forcing a shudder to spread across my shoulders. 'I'm sure I'll be absolutely fine, honestly.'

Liam

We're both perched on the doormat, staring at the front door. The key hangs there in the lock, about to turn, its teeth nestled between the grooves and jutting out from the flat surface of the door. She's distraught. Cut up by what she's had to endure in one afternoon. I can hardly say I blame her, but I don't think it's a good idea to be going into her flat. I really need to get back to work or, at least, not be in a stranger's home.

It's just I can't bring myself to leave her, I can't make myself walk away. The thought of actually going into her flat, even if it is just for a quick cup of tea, makes me feel ill, repulsed at myself for abusing her trust or whatever it is I'd be doing. It feels wrong, going in this woman's home after what she's told me, but I can't move. She's magnetic. I don't feel like she's leaving me any choice.

Besides, she's terrified.

Eventually I relent and nod. 'I can come in for one. I'll need to let work know where I am though.'

'Of course,' she says.

She turns the key.

'Welcome home.' She flashes me a grin over her shoulder, but it doesn't translate quite right in her eyes.

Welcome home.

Sarah

He walks in behind me, stands in the hallway and waits for my direction. Obedient. I indicate to the living room with a nod. He naturally gravitates to the chair that I bought for him. I'm thrilled he likes it. He'll look good in it.

'How do you take your tea?' I ask, leaning against the doorframe as if this scene is normal, as if it happens everyday.

'Milk, no sugar please.'

He hovers in the living room by the chair, looking slightly out of place.

'Please, feel free to sit down. Make yourself at home,' I say as I motion to the navy blue armchair. He sits, legs crossed at the knee. He looks a little nervous, but that will pass I'm sure. I lean my head on the doorframe and just stare at the back of his head, at his dark hair, at the wisps of chocolate brown that curl up behind his ears. It's all so familiar but so alien, to have him sitting in my home. To have him that bit closer than I've ever managed to have him before. I can't believe he's actually here–he's finally here. I take him in, drink him up with my eyes as the kettle boils and whistles in the background.

He's in. And that means he's mine.

I'm in the kitchen making tea. I grab two mugs, the matching grey and white ones I've bought specifically for us as a couple. They complement each other perfectly, stood side by side about an inch apart and an inch away from the edge of the work surface. A tea bag slumps into each mug, curved against the rounded bottom of the cup. I pour over boiling water and watch the bag as it bleeds into the clear liquid, drowning it with colour. I splash in the milk then squeeze the bag and give each mug a stir.

I catch a quick glance back into the living and find him still sitting there, hunched and tense. He's right where I want him, but he looks so unnatural. This isn't going to be as easy as I'd hoped. I don't want to startle him. It's probably best to ease him in gently, to give him a gentle helping hand.

I slide his mug away from my own and push a cluster of white pills into the liquid. They disappear almost instantly, floating on the surface for a millisecond before drifting to the bottom. I swirl the tea around to make sure they've fully dissolved. I tap the spoon on the side of each mug, making a satisfying clink and walk the tea through to the living room. He cradles the steaming mug between his hands. He still looks nervous, but the warm mug seems to have alleviated some of the tension. It's beginning to annoy me, this insistence on being uncomfortable. If he just gave in and loosened up, it wouldn't be necessary for me to play the next part of this sequence, but he's left me no choice. It's quite sad, I suppose. Watching him act like an abused or neglected pet when, really, I'm opening up my home to him. He ought to be grateful.

My familiar armchair welcomes the weight of my body with a gentle sigh as I lower myself amongst the cushions and fold my legs.

'Thank you again, really,' I say, sipping the tea. 'I do feel so much better.'

'Not a problem at all. Are you sure you'll be okay? I don't want to leave you until you're sure.' *Oh, you won't be leaving.* It's a strange choice of words for someone whose face is telling such a contrasting story. His face is pained and awkward and ill at ease, yet his words attempt a different version of the truth.

'I'll be fine, Noah, thank you, though.' My tongue trips over his name; I really don't like it. 'Actually, would you mind if I borrowed your phone just to let my Mum know I'm home. She knows what happened, but my battery has died. I just want to send her a quick text.'

He hands me his mobile without even thinking. I pretend to use it, tapping away at the screen, and place it down on the coffee table between us. He doesn't retrieve it and goes back to sipping his tea.

I feel strangely relaxed now he's in the flat, but I know deep down the work is just beginning. I know we'll probably have some teething issues at first, but what good relationship doesn't have a few spats at the beginning? That's what makes you stronger, getting through those arguments; they're what make us all human.

'So, what is it you do for a living?' I ask, though I know the answer full well. I let him answer, I let him talk his job up to me, and I let him be impressed with himself for a few minutes though I see right through him. He's stuck in a reasonably paid corporate job. Though the money is good, he hates it. It makes the world and everything in it seem grey and cold. Not that mine is any better.

'I'm just a secretary, really. A P.A. to one of the CEO's over at the medical research charity just over the road from your place. It's not much, but it pays the bills and gives me the time I need to do the things I love.'

I'm talking at him now, really. His eyes are glazing over, a frosty curtain drifting across his irises and he's looking straight through me rather than at me. The pill is grabbing at the nerves behind his eyes, dragging away his focus and attention. He squints and shuts his eyes tight against the intensifying fatigue. He's drowsy. He looks quite sweet so sleepy and unaware.

'I really love to read and travel with my family, you know? All the usual stuff, really. This year has been hard, but I think it's just made me stronger.' I'm reeling off the rehearsed lines, throwing the clichés at him as he loses concentration. I've practiced these so many times; I know exactly what to say. 'Where is it you said your family was from?'

He looks at me, startled. He just about heard the question, but he is struggling to process the answer, much less muster the energy to speak. The drugs are spreading their tendrils, curling and grasping at his limbs and his eyelids.

'Uh, I don't think I did mention where they were from. They're, I mean, they live out in, erm, Oxfordshire. Quite a way from here.'

Yawns litter his speech and his head is lulling to the side, weighed down by exhaustion. He's really fighting this. I stay quiet for a minute and just watch him. His eyelids drag over his irises, opening and closing in slow motion, exaggerating every movement. I'm quite impressed actually–he's really battling the urge to sleep much longer than I usually manage. It doesn't take him too long though. A few minutes of sitting and letting the silence surround him and his head has finally dropped, dripping the last pool of tea into his lap.

Moving him is harder than I could have imagined. Sleep has claimed him surprisingly quickly and his muscles and limbs fill with cement as he dead weights, sinking further into the armchair. His face is peaceful and serene but looks awkward next to his ungainly limbs. I struggle to lift him only a few centimetres from the floor, dragging him from the chair and into our bedroom. His feet scrape against the floor as I lunge and pull his unconscious body into the next room. Luckily he's out cold; he won't feel a thing.

I heave him up onto the bed, pulling his legs onto the divan and stretching him out. His hands fall naturally at his sides, resting softly on the duvet. I take a few moments to gaze at him, to stare at his face, to finally appreciate what we have. I can't believe I'm just inches away from him. He's even more beautiful this close up. I stare at him for minutes, memorizing each and every inch of his face, every freckle, and dimple of his skin. I trace my fingers over his body, committing every tiny detail to memory. His energy hovers and crackles above his torso as I drift my palms across his skin. My fingers prickle across the white buttons of his shirt, writhing across the fabric of the pressed cotton as it flows over his abdomen. Each button gives a slight tug as it's released, revealing his perfect, alabaster skin. The shirt shrugs off his body, and I tug it from under his shoulders. He's exactly as I'd imagined. Pale skin, not a single blemish. Chiselled, muscular torso, smooth angular shoulders, and sharp, masculine collarbones. His belt slides easily from the loops in his chinos and thuds onto the floor. His presence in my home, on my bed, makes me shudder. The excitement of it is almost overwhelming; I've never felt anything like it. Every decision I've made, and every decision I will ever make is because of him—because of the love I feel for him. The power and control it has over me is unnerving. I fight to stay in control.

I pull the new set of pyjamas over his head, tugging them across his body and up around his waist. The whole process is much more romantic in my head, but in reality, it's quite awkward and ungainly. He'll thank me, I'm sure. I've woken too many times in my work clothes, and it's not comfortable at all. I shuffle his body over to the other side of the bed, his side, and lay his head onto the feather pillow. The duvet rests just under his chin, caressing his neck and cheeks. He is so still and so peaceful and breathing so gently that he could pass for dead if you looked too quickly. I lay next to him for a few minutes, just to see what it feels like. I place my hand on his chest, spreading each finger out as far as I can reach to feel his heartbeat strong and regular through the thin t-shirt. My face is inches from his; my nose just brushes his cheek, breathing in the smooth, warm scent of sandalwood. He smells familiar and homely. I lay a kiss on his cheek and witness the electricity between us again. The sparks are so real I can almost see them. I lift myself gently off the bed and leave him to rest, pulling the door closed behind me.

Chapter Eleven

Liam.

My hands are on her skin - smooth, porcelain-like and unbelievably soft to the touch. Her hair drapes across my face, lying in strands over my nose and tickling my cheeks. I drift gradually to consciousness, like a ball floating to the surface of a deep pool of water, buoyant and bobbing. Everything is moving in slow motion, ethereal and surreal. My body is curled around hers, a protective layer from the outside world. Her chest and back rise and fall, brushing against my torso with every breath. My arms are wrapped around her body, our fingers interlaced. I can feel her skin against mine. It feels electric but relaxed, new but natural. Who is this beautiful woman and when did I get so, so lucky? Her hair brushes my face as it moves with my breath.

I lay with my eyes closed for a while longer, allowing myself to stay in this beautifully relaxed setting. I don't want to open my eyes to find this has all been a dream.

She's stirring, shuffling and shifting in the bed next to me, nestling her face deeper into the pillow. I roll over as gently as possible to free my arm, now flooding with pins and needles. I give in and open my eyes.

I'm staring at a ceiling I don't recognise, in a room I've never been in before. I stay quiet, trying to wake myself from what I thought was another layer of a dream. It's dark outside, the dusty blue sky peering through a slit in the curtains, an orange-lit street lamp throwing eerie shadows across the room. It's only half a window really—a narrow slit of glass offering a vision of the outside world. Half a window, offering half a view of half a street-lamp and half a pathway cut in half horizontally by a wall. The view is cut up further by what looks like metal bars, cold and slightly rusty.

Am I in someone's basement? A basement flat, I suppose. *Stay calm, Noah, breathe.* I have no recollection of how I got here. My eyes dart frantically around the room, but I keep my torso as still as possible so as not to wake the woman next to me. My limbs are heavy, my hands and feet thick and struggling to wake up from a weighty, numb sleep. The room looks freshly decorated, like a showroom or an image from a home magazine. I don't recognise the wardrobes. I don't recognise the bedding. I don't recognise the curtains or the window or the walls or the furnishings or the ceiling or the door. I don't know where I am.

I can smell paint. Fresh paint and newly unpackaged bedding and I'm wearing clothes I have never seen before. They're not mine. The clothes I am currently wearing do not belong to me, and I don't know how I'm wearing them or where they came from. They're coarse on my skin as if unwashed, or fresh from a packet. I don't recall changing. I don't know where my actual clothes are, or where any of my things are. My heart pounds in my chest, thudding against my rib cage as if trying to escape. There must be a logical explanation for this. I don't remember going to a bar or, or getting drunk. Hell, I haven't touched alcohol for months.

The last thing I can remember is—is her. I remember her so well. My eyes fall down to the face of the woman I know is lying motionless beside me. What have I done?

I jerk my head back, waking her up. I can't hide my shock; it spreads across my face like wildfire. I rack my brain for her name, for any solid recollection or memory of who this person is and what she might be to me.

'Sarah?'

She looks up and smiles at me. Her hair falls in dark waves across my chest, the ends matted from sleep. She leans forward and kisses me slowly on the lips. My body tenses as her mouth makes contact with mine, and I try to move away from her.

'What's wrong?' Her tone is full of disappointment. Her face is torn and broken as I reject her. She's surprised by my reaction, as if she hasn't a clue that something isn't right here.

'Sarah, this is wrong, I--,' I trail off. I don't know what I'm trying to say. I'm not sure why I'm trying to say it. Something feels off.

She interrupts my speech with another kiss, slower, more deliberate and as much as I try, I can't stop myself from kissing her back. Something feels very off, but I can't stop myself. I let myself lean into her, pushing against her warm, damp lips. I run my hand through her hair and breathe in her sweet, floral perfume and try my best to recall some memory of what has happened. She pulls away, holding my chin in her hands and smiles again.

'Don't worry, it's just a bit of fun. It was just what I needed. Thank you,' she said, with a glint in her eye and a slightly smug look spread across her face. 'Wait here, I'll grab us a coffee.'

I do as she says. I don't know why. I could just as easily get up and walk out, but for some reason I don't feel like I want to. I still can't quite work out what has happened or how it has happened or how it could possibly have slipped my mind. But she intrigues me, so I decide to stay. She seems surprisingly unoffended by the whole situation.

I prop myself up on the mound of pillows and cushions and try to take in the room properly now the light is on. The walls are covered in photographs, images of Sarah's family, much the same as the ones in the living room and the hallway. They look slightly odd, slightly familiar, but I can't place where I've seen them before. It takes me a while to notice, but she isn't in any of the photos. There are fresh brush strokes sweeping the walls, barely noticeable grooves streaking the paint. It all feels very new.

Moments later she wanders back in, shuffling across the floor in a peach silk negligee and hands me a steaming cup of tea.

'Honestly, Noah, it doesn't matter. It was just a bit of fun. Don't look so worried,' she says as she slides back under the covers next to me. Her leg wraps around mine, her skin smooth and cool against my calf.

Not a single memory of the event that quite clearly took place in this stranger's bed surfaces in my mind, and I hope desperately that she can't read the confusion on my face. I need to get out of here.

'Just relax and enjoy it, don't worry yourself,' she says, grinning at me.

The nagging black hole in my memory isn't filling any time soon; in fact, it seems to be widening. I'm anxious and irritable; my brain itches as I desperately try to remember something - anything. I can't just lay here and act like this is normal–like I feel okay with whatever has gone on. 'Sarah, I'm so sorry. I--I really can't remember what happened,' I say, dragging my body up under the duvet so I'm in a seated position. 'What time is it?'

'It's just gone seven thirty. And as for what happened–I must say, I'm slightly disappointed that you don't remember. How about I remind you?'

She lifts the tea from my grasp, placing it on the bedside cabinet beside me and swings her leg over my torso, leaning down and kissing my neck. Her hot breath sweeps over my throat as she kisses behind my ear. I'm inches away from giving into her, but I can't. Not knowing what she's been through. I'm not like that. I can't take advantage of her.

'Sarah, sorry–no,' I say, placing my hands on her shoulders and pushing her away. Her arms are slim but toned and I can feel the curvature of her bones beneath the skin. 'I'm really sorry, I–I can't do this. Where are my clothes? Where are my things? I need to leave.'

'I understand, Liam. Please just stay, just for a while?'

I frown at the mention of someone else's name. Maybe that's the name of the ex-boyfriend–the one that injured her hand. We've only known each other a matter of hours, so I suppose it's a genuine slip of the tongue but the mistake just encourages me to leave. 'Noah,' I say, starting to swing my legs out of the bed. 'My name is Noah.'

'Yes, sorry,' she replies, shuffling under the covers. I look over and face her. Her eyes are pleading with me. I can't just walk out, not knowing what she's been through, but I can't stay either. Even if she's more than happy to spend more time in my company, I feel dirty–awful–for taking advantage of her. I'm not that kind of person, this isn't me and I know I need to leave.

'Just sit down,' she says, laying her hand on my leg. 'Just stay for a few more minutes,' she begs, squeezing her fingers into my thigh. Her eyes drill straight into mine, pleading and filling with silent tears.

I relent and sit back on the bed, forcing myself to try and remember anything from the previous five or six hours. She slides up behind me, wrapping her legs around my torso and massages my shoulders, rolling and dragging her thumbs and knuckles into my skin. She pauses for a few seconds, placing her head in the curve of my neck and plants a few butterfly kisses over my shoulder.

'You're really tense,' she whispers. 'I've got something stronger than tea if you like?'

I shouldn't have sat back down. I'm itchy and anxious and inches away from losing it. I don't want to hurt her, not any more than she's already been hurt today.

I turn to face her and place my hand gently on her shoulder.

'Sarah, look, I'm really sorry. I really think I should go, okay?' Once I start talking the words come flooding out, spilling onto my chest. The more I say it aloud, the more I realise I need to leave. Now. 'I can come back later? I'm happy to talk if you need me, but I really think I ought to go and let you think this through. It's been a really hard day. I don't want to take advantage.'

To be honest, I think I'm the one who needs to think it through.

Her eyes don't leave mine the entire time I'm talking. Her jaw tenses, the tendons stiffening and jutting out from her cheeks. I think I've embarrassed her, humiliated her, but she finally gives in to what I'm asking.

'Wait here. I'll go and get your things', she says as she stands up to leave the bedroom. She climbs out of the bed, her legs brushing against me and groans as she bends down to grab a dressing gown. I watch her back as she leaves.

Sarah.

I leave the room slowly, acting hurt and forlorn and a little dejected. I take my time and force the best victim face across my features that I can muster. I'm not letting him leave; I've just got him here. I love him. We could be so happy together – we will be. I'm furious that he can't even see that, but I understand. It's all moved so fast. I shouldn't have expected him to keep up – I expected far too much of him.

And of course, nothing actually happened once I'd put him to bed. I wandered around for a while, made some precautions. His belongings are in a small safe that I bought in the cupboard in the hallway. I've taken the battery out of his phone and hidden that separately, just in case he manages to find it. I've stashed away any old belonging of his that will point to his old life and replaced them with other things – better things – that I've bought just for him. The shoes that I took off him when he fell asleep are gone, replaced with the better ones that I specifically chose for him. His jacket is in the safe, along with his old clothes and any indication of who he once was. He'll thank me later.

It's a shame he's put me in this position, really. I gave him the perfect chance to wake up, blissfully happy next to me, accepting our new relationship and settling into new routines. But he's made it expressly clear that he doesn't want that. He wants to leave. After everything I've already done for him, after all I've sacrificed and changed about myself and he still wants to leave. I can't let him do that, so, unfortunately, we're going to have to do this the hard way. It really is such a shame. I gave him a chance, but there's nothing else I can do– he's left me no choice. This is his fault, and I'll be sure to tell him later on down the line when he's not happy with me.

I toyed with a few different ideas when going through these scenarios in my head last night. I knew deep down that it wouldn't be easy, but I'd held onto a tiny sliver of hope that he'd actually want me, that he'd be happy to stay. I thought of all sorts of different options: drugs, violence, straight up kidnapping and tying him to something solid and heavy so he couldn't escape, having the windows barred up. I really did want to give him the best opportunity to let this happen naturally, but now I know that can't happen. I tried to be the good person here, to let things happen as they should, but I know that that's not an option I have the luxury of selecting.

He's fumbling around in the bedroom, looking for his things. He won't find any of them in there, that's for sure. I drag the next step of my plan out for a few more moments, listening in to him shuffling around on the new carpet. I'll let him enjoy his freedom, just for a minute more. I love how confused he looked when he woke up, how concerned he was that he couldn't remember what he did this afternoon, how desperately he's racking his memory for a fragment, for a tiny clue of what he thinks he's guilty of. Of course, he never actually did anything, but I'm not going to be the one to tell him that. I need to maintain this leverage over him. I can hear him moving about, shifting things, opening the drawers of the new cabinets to find the packing and dust sheets still in them, sliding the wardrobe doors open to find nothing but a few shirts hanging inside. I didn't consider how confusing it would be to wake up in a freshly painted box, but I thought I'd be enough to convince him to stay. Maybe he's even checking under the bed for the precious belongings from his past life. Oh, I hope he is seriously racking his brains for any memory, anything to indicate what he has spent the last few hours doing. The more confused he is, the easier it will be for me to convince him that he needs to stay. I let him rummage for a few seconds longer, the newly caged, confused animal. He'll understand soon enough.

The fumbling stops. The silence that replaces it is eerie and tense, the whole flat holding its breath. Excitement builds in me like electricity as I strain my ears for any tiny sound that he might make. I tease a saucepan off the shelf behind me. My fingers curl around the handle, adrenaline buzzing through my palms. It's cold and smooth, coursing with energy. The door to our bedroom opens just a crack, to reveal Liam peering around sheepishly. I'm hidden just out of sight behind the kitchen door, but I can see him through the gap where the door meets the frame, still wearing his new pyjamas. The pan feels heavy in my hand–a solution I wasn't aware I'd have to come to until it had already started to happen. The hallway light catches his blue eyes and reminds me why I'm doing this. I watch, soundlessly, as he steps out of the room onto the hallway carpet.

'Sarah?' He calls out to me. 'I really ought to go.'

I hold my breath like a small child playing hide and seek, trying not to give away my position. I don't want to let him in on my next surprise—that would ruin it for both of us. That would ruin everything. I can't chance giving him the upper hand, not after all the work I've put into this already. I'm waiting. He's standing in the hallway, questioning which way to go. He edges towards the kitchen. My grip tightens around the handle of the pan as I prise it from the work surface, every sound magnified in the still silence until my skin brushing against the metal handle is almost deafening. Any second now.

'Sarah, come on,' he says, his voice emanating just feet away from the kitchen door.

I take a step closer, the pan now hanging at my side, the cool metal sending a shiver up my bare leg.

I've never been this close to having someone love me back. To having someone look me in the eye, feeling what I feel for them in its truest form. Of course, I've loved other people before, plenty of times, actually. But it's never been reciprocated in this way. I've never had the chance to make that person feel for me the way I feel for them. I can't let that opportunity drift away from me.

His hand is on the door. I can sense it, his palm touching the wood, his pulse thudding and sending the blood coursing up his wrist and into the tips of his fingers. It's casting a long, thin shadow through the crack onto the kitchen floor. I've stopped breathing.

'Sarah?' The door inches open in slow motion, teasing me, taunting me, flirting with my will power. I can't open it; I need to let him come to me. I'm stood a few feet behind the swing of the door, wielding the pan, waiting for him to come in. The next few seconds drag on, mocking me and testing my patience.

He's finally here, finally facing me. I let myself look at his face for only a second. I can't afford to let myself think about it, or I might choke, or worse, he could bolt. Don't make eye contact; don't question your decision, just think of your love for him. Do what needs to be done. Think only of the end goal. This is his fault. He has made you do this.

I swing the pan and brace myself as the flat metal rushes to meet his skull. A loud, sharp crack fills the kitchen as the metal connects with his head. He stumbles, legs crossing, eyes wide and frantic. I stand back as he tries to grab the edge of the work surface to steady his swaying body. One hand fumbles for the worktop, the other instinctively flies up to his head. His muscular body remains upright as I prepare myself to have another go. My lips stretch across my face in a smile I can only imagine looks manic to him. The pan glints in the fluorescent kitchen lights as I hold it high above my head and wait for him to make eye contact with me. The horror spills from his eyes, glistening in the incandescent glow. His face begs for mercy, willing me to stop. The pan comes down harder and faster this time, splitting the air in two and slamming into the crown of his head. A hysterical laugh escapes my chest as a gong rings out from the pan. His knees give way to his weight as his body crashes down. His joints slacken like overstretched elastic, leaving his limbs to tumble to the ground as he rests in a heap, the shadow of the pan stretched out across his face.

'I am sorry, but you didn't leave me any choice.'

I place the pan on the kitchen counter and kneel by his side. His face is warm, and his limbs are caught under his body in an awkward, tangled bundle. I place two fingers on his throat, finding a pulse and run my hands through his hair to check for any lasting damage. It wasn't my aim to really hurt him, but I needed to knock some sense into him. I just need some more time to convince him that he needs to stay, that's all. It's important that I let him know I'm in charge at this early stage. I'm the one who'll be making the decisions from now on, and it's best for everyone that he gets used to that.

I watch him for a while, crumpled on the floor like a puppet whose strings have been cut loose. He's beautifully still, like a fallen flower petal. There's no sign of pain on his face; I find comfort in that. He lays perfectly still except for the flutter of his heart as it pulsates in his neck. I don't want to move him just yet, he looks so comfortable and at peace. His face is so innocent, unmarred and wholesome. I watch him like a mother looks at their first-born child, with nothing but overwhelming love. My desire to protect him and keep him as my own is crushing. I brush my hand over his cheek and gently kiss his cool lips.

I know the time has come to move him again, before he has a chance to regain consciousness. I grab him under his armpits and drag his heavy frame into the living room, using the weight of my own body to heave him across the carpeted floor. I lunge and lean against my own weight to shift him to the next room, the muscles in my thighs protesting against his strong and muscular frame. His body is stretched out on the living floor with his arms resting by his side.

Everything I'll need to begin the process is there, laid out on the table. Each item settled in its own space, resting between invisible grid lines. Three lengths of strong rope knotted and curled, handcuffs and a soaked rag all waiting their turn in the ritual. Lifting his body into the chair is a struggle. I assumed he'd be quite heavy, but I still struggle against his weight, heaving and balancing his body against the wooden back so he doesn't roll onto the floor.

I start with his hands. I place them together behind his back, cuffing them and slipping the hoop of the cuff through one of the bars on the back of the chair. It pays to be cautious. I tie each ankle to each leg of the chair, pulling the rope as tight as I can so his shins are pulled parallel to the wooden legs. I slip some rope around his torso, over his stomach and through the slats in the back of the chair. Such a sad, unfortunate thing, he's made me do. How much easier this would have been if he'd just played along, if he'd just made a bit more of an effort. I've found that, throughout my life, I'm always the one to make the first move, to put in the most effort. His eyes flutter under his eyelids, but he doesn't come-to. Not just yet. I pry his mouth open, pulling against his stiff and heavy jaw. I grab the rag of tattered fabric and place it between his teeth, pushing it gently towards the back of his throat.

'Now Liam, this would have been so much easier if you'd have just relaxed and stopped worrying,' I say, leaning down by his lap, my hands on his knees. 'Now look what you've made me do. I hope you realise you were the one to put me in this position.'

I straighten the ropes across his torso, neatening up the ties. 'You really left me no choice, so you'd better not blame me for this. If you'd just stopped worrying, this would have been so much easier. But don't worry. I'll help you through it. We'll get through it together. You'll see. I'll be right here when you wake up.'

I step away and watch him, unconscious and heavy against the chair. I really hope he does understand.

This is what we do for love.

Chapter Twelve

I've always found laying the table for dinner so therapeutic. Instructions as follows: clear the table, wipe over with a damp cloth to get rid of any flecks of last night's food. Not that there are any signs of that given that the table was only delivered yesterday. Next, wipe over with an alternative, dry cloth. No one likes damp elbows or smeared tables; how ungainly that would be, to have to suffer through a whole meal with wet patches on your sleeves. Once the table is dry, lay out the placemats. One for each person, so in this instance just two, and a smaller, square mat for the glass of wine. It has to be precise, like a surgical procedure.

We're not having starters today. I couldn't bring myself to cook three courses, not after having eaten microwave meals for months. Two courses would be quite enough. Oh, and then there's the cutlery. Polish it in the kitchen. Plunge it in boiling hot water and then rub it dry quickly with a thick cloth to get the best shine. You can feel the heat pulsating under the cloth, but it doesn't bite through the fabric. Lay it around the placemats, knife on the right, fork on the left, dessert fork and spoon facing opposite directions at the top of the place setting. No cutting corners–it looks better if you do it right. I fetch a cool bottle of white wine from the fridge, uncork it and set it down in the centre of the table, supported by a wine glass on either side and a small tumbler of cool water each.

I step back and take a look at my work. I know it's not much to any normal person, but this is our first meal together as a couple, and I'm determined to make it right. Even if it tastes horrific, we'll have each other's company and some good wine to get us through the evening. I've even bought linen napkins and rolled them up tightly in pretty, floral napkin rings. A single candle is in the middle of the table, flickering and glowing against the warm lighting in the living room, throwing shadows over the neck of the wine bottle, stretching the droplets of condensation to the bottom. No effort is too great for him.

Now all I can do is wait for him to come to.

I can't take my eyes off of him. He's propped up opposite me at the table, bound to the chair with a sturdy length of rope, reams of silver duct tape and the handcuffs I purchased online. I'll give him time to wake up on his own. After what he's been through today, the sleep is probably doing him good. I'll just sit here, sipping my wine, and wait for him to wake up.

Liam

I can hear her. Her silhouette shifts and moves around in the room, a shuffling figure just visible through the thin film of my eyelids. I try to follow the shape of her with my eyes, but she leaves the room again, just out of my reach. I follow her shadow as far as my eyes will let me, the tendons pulling taught and protesting to the movement. The pain is excruciating. It's at its worst when I move my eyes too quickly. The motion sends tiny shards of glass spraying through my arteries, peppering my brain. I'm drowsy and heavy, my conscience and mind sluggish and lethargic. The pain has clamped my eyelids shut and sealed them tight. I'm not fully aware of where I am or what has happened in the last few hours. I just know that I am in pain, floating in and out of consciousness, drifting in and out of the worst sleep I've ever had. Something rough is pushing down on my tongue, some kind of fabric or cloth. It's swollen and wet and clogs every inch of my mouth, forcing my jaw open. I try to swallow, but the motion thrusts the fabric against the back of my throat, the cloth scraping the sensitive skin as my stomach and diaphragm contract. I manage to silence the retching, but I can't swallow at all with the cloth in the way. I can hardly breathe. It takes all of my concentration not to gag. My hands are yanked behind me, forcing my shoulder blades to twist in on themselves. Cold metal is digging into the skin of my wrists, and there's more rope holding my shoulders down against the back of the wooden chair. The sharp angles of the chair dig into the flesh behind my kneecaps, grating against the small bones as I shift my weight.

There is a small, inaudible voice mumbling in the dark, just below the surface of my consciousness. It's a woman's voice, soft and slurred, interjected with shorter, sharper phrases. It bounces around, hopping in and out of my concentration like flies on the top of a pond. It's almost as if the woman is instructing herself under her breath, telling someone off, perhaps. I know it's her. I can feel her in the darkness waiting for her next move, prowling around the flat waiting for the first sign of weakness to pounce on. It will only be a matter of time until my eyes drift open and throw me back into the harsh reality of this flat, of Sarah's home. I'm going to drag out the inevitability for as long as possible.

The voice gets louder; it's much closer now. She's back in the room, hovering around the table and moving things around again. There's the clink of glasses, the brush of fabric as she sweeps her hand across the place settings, the acidic, unmistakeably vinegary scent of wine. I will not open my eyes. I'm floating back to reality, inches away from the surface. I can smell her; I can see her staring at me through the papery thinness of my eyelids. I can feel her watching me as I inhale, exhale. I bob around the surface of consciousness like a buoy on the tide.

The image of her lifting the pan over her head ready to strike me flashes behind my eyes - her face twisted, manic, full of madness. She knew what she was doing; she'd calculated this whole thing. She must be sick. She's terrified of someone else betraying her, so she's made sure that I can't. I will not open my eyes. I'll let her think she's done some serious damage, let her panic for a while. Then she'll have to realise how insane this all is, ring an ambulance and pretend the whole thing was an accident. I'll play along for a while. But I'll be gone, away from here, and that's all I care about.

The pain in my head is increasing with the smell of the wine. I've never known pain quite like it. A sharp needle burns a hole through my skull, scorching and blazing behind my retinas. I need to slow my breathing. If I inhale in too fast,

I think I'll choke on the rag filling up my mouth and swelling against my teeth.

She's still talking, but she's moved again, her voice ebbing and drifting away. I can't zone in on exactly what she is saying, but I think she's talking to me. Concentrating hurts too much to do it for too long, but she is definitely talking directly at me now. I flinch as long fingers spread out across my knee.

'Liam? Come on now, it's time to wake up,' her voice whispers, its timbre thin and ethereal.

Liam?

The words flitter around my face, just on the edge of my conscience. They're spacy and watery and hard to completely hone in on, like each letter is slightly too far apart and spoken too slowly. She leaves enough of a gap after each sentence, as if waiting for me to reply.

'Liam. It's time.'

She can't be talking to me.

'I've worked for hours on this meal for us. Are you just going to doze through the whole thing?'

Her voice is calm, but it's laced with a threatening, serious undertone that sends shivers up my spine.

Keep your eyes closed. Make her think she's really hurt you. Focus. Focus on breathing slowly and steadily.

I clamp my eyelids shut as tight as I can.

'Liam,' the whispering voice sings.

Her hand spreads over my knee, the tips of her fingers pressing into my flesh.

'You really don't want to make me angry. Not after what I've been through already. Just open your eyes and see what I've done for you,' she hisses.

Her words hang in the air, suspended above my head, dangling there like a guillotine blade. I don't respond. I don't open my eyes. I refuse.

Her hand is on my face. I jump, I felt myself do it. Maybe she didn't notice.

Pray she didn't.

I clamp my eyes shut and slow my breathing as much as I can without making it noticeable, but my nostrils flare. I can feel each tiny crease surrounding my eyes, the tiny details that will give me away. My face is glowing red-hot. Her breath is stroking my cheeks, warm and damp - her nose and her lips centimetres away from mine.

I've stopped breathing. I can't afford to panic - I know I can't trust this woman. Everything, every inch of my body, every hair and every pore has tensed, bracing for impact. My skin is crawling, every cell so receptive to her movements, so on edge. Her hair is tickling my neck, brushing against my skin. I can't wake up.

Do not wake up.

Every beat of my heart is thunderous against my chest. I wonder if she can hear it, I wonder if she can hear my hair follicles clambering on my skin.

Focus, Noah, focus on keeping your eyes closed. She's not onto you. She doesn't know that you're conscious. Just last a few more minutes. Any second now she'll step away.

Any second now.

Sarah

He's adorable, toying with me. His eyes are darting behind their lids, flitting to and from, fighting to stay clamped closed against the light. I'll test him. See just how much he can resist me.

My face is millimetres from his, just breathing in his scent. He's trying to fight it, but any second now he'll give in and his eyes will open. The arteries and tendons are pulled taught down his neck, his jaw tensing and flexing as he tries to control his breathing. He thinks I can't see it, but I see everything. Every muscle, every ounce of flesh tightening, rigid against his throat.

Any second now.

Any second and he'll give up. He'll have to.

This is boring me now. He's lasted a lot longer than I imagined he would. I kiss him square on the lips in the hope that that will shake him out of this catatonic state, but it doesn't. I end up kissing a pair of cold, unresponsive lips. Not so much as a flinch. I can't be bothered to sit here and wait for him any longer. I've slaved over the perfect meal for him, and now he doesn't even have the decency to be awake to enjoy it with me.

I give up. I won't let him humiliate me like this.

I leave him be for a few more minutes, bringing the plates from the kitchen out onto the table. The smell of the food does nothing to bring him to. I waft it under his nose, dragging the plates through the air. Nothing. It's irritating me now. A grunt escapes my throat as I slam the plate down in front of him, frustration rising in my chest.

'How dare you be so ungrateful?'

I'm shouting to myself, still no reaction from him whatsoever.

After everything I've done for him, how dare he be so rude. I redecorated my home. I rearranged my entire life to accommodate him, brought him his own furniture and belongings to make him feel at ease and feel safe. I changed everything about myself for him. And he's pretending to be out-cold, so he doesn't have to face me. His ungratefulness disgusts me. I can't bring myself to look at him, I can't accept that I brought this man into my home, I welcomed him, sacrificed everything for him.

I refuse to think I've made the wrong choice. Liam is perfect. This is just a lapse in his judgement, an impulsive act.

'What an idiot!'

I scream as I bring my open palm across his face again, his eyes finally opening. A guttural, animalistic shriek floods from my mouth as I grab his chin, wrenching his face up towards the light. I shock even myself with the volume and intensity of it and catch myself halfway through yelling his name at him.

'Liam!' I howl into the silent room. I register his confusion; the fear in his features underlined by his bewilderment. And then it hits me. 'Oh, I'm so sorry, I forgot to tell you. I've been calling you Liam all this time and expecting you to understand and respond to me.' A hysterical giggle escapes my lips. I lean on the table to steady myself as my sides ache with the laughter. 'What a ridiculous situation we've found ourselves in! What an oversight!' The laughter continues—I can't make it stop. No wonder he's not been responding to me for all this time. I catch my breath and try my best to explain.

'I don't like Noah. The name, I mean. It doesn't sound right next to mine. So it's Liam from now on.' I wait for him to show that he's understood, but it's clear that he hasn't. He just wears this perplexed look, eyebrows slightly tilted, eyes squinting.

'Liam? Are we clear?' Still nothing, no words to reassure me. 'What don't you understand?' I'm in his face again now, squatting down beside him. 'It's not a hard concept. What are you struggling?'

His jaw has clamped down, shutting his tongue away in a protest of silence. It's not that he doesn't understand my point of view, it's that he's refusing to even comprehend the situation. And now he's refusing to speak to me, refusing to let me in. I can't be shut out like this; the whole thing makes me feel hideously desperate.

'Oh, Liam, I'm so *so* sorry for hurting you. Again. God, I really am so sorry. If only I'd realised earlier and explained it all to you. Then we wouldn't be in this mess.'

I give in and fuss over him for a while, but he winces and tries to pull his head away from me. I run my hands over his face and try to hide the pity in my eyes, but he's so confused that I can't help but feel a little sorry for him. But I do also find it a little humorous, how I can have such a huge impact on this strong, muscular man. We're all weak underneath it all.

I've resigned to the fact that he's not going to engage me in conversation just yet. But there's no use wasting my efforts, so I sit and begin eating. His face pulls into a grimace, contorted and pained. He stares at me as I eat, his face full of wonder.

'Now Liam, I can't trust you to have your own knife and fork. How silly do you think I am?'

I shift around into the chair next to him. I grab the cutlery that's placed in front of him and cut up his food. I like the feeling that I'm looking after him and make a real point of cutting it slowly, deliberately. He relies on me for everything now, and I crave that feeling of responsibility. That feeling that without me, Liam would whither and starve and be left to rot. I cut the food into cubes, sliding a piece onto the fork and offering it to him. I imagine us, like those two dogs in that Disney movie, romantically feeding each other, looking longingly into each other's eyes. I pull the rag from his mouth, watching as he gasps and tries not to gag. I press the small chunk to his lips, waiting for them to part, but he turns his head away from me, trying to shake me away.

'Being ungrateful again, are we?'

He holds his head away from me, looking down at the floor.

'I cooked this especially for you.' I might as well be speaking to myself. He doesn't turn his head to look at me, doesn't even acknowledge that I'm still here. I sit back and purse my lips.

'It's because I love you.' I don't mean to say it so early on, but it just sort of slips out naturally. It felt like the right time for me to say it and the right time for Liam to hear it. I say it just loud enough for him to hear me and the truth of the statement hits me as it escapes my lips.

'You *love* me?' He's the one staring at me now, his voice filling with bewilderment and disbelief. His eyebrows furrow, his face twists into an image equal parts confusion and horror. 'Do you even know what love is? Are you absolutely insane?'

'Don't call me that', I say, shaking my head. It's not the first time I've had that insult thrown at me, but I've learnt not to take it. Not from anyone.

'You attacked me!' He's yelling now. I can't have him yelling, even if the flats above are empty, it's not something I'm willing to risk. I grab the rag from the corner of the table and thrust it back into his mouth, pressing it against the back of his throat. He thrashes his head about to try to stop me, and I clamp my fingertips into the sides of his jaw. He tries to throw me off, but I manage to force it into his mouth all the same. He underestimates me.

I've still got my fingers clamped into his neck, his Adam's apple forcing its way down his throat and grating against my grasp.

'Because I love you! You were going to leave. I had to show you that I love you!' I'm yelling at him now, trying my hardest to get him to understand. I'm standing over the table screeching almost inaudibly at him, my hands balled into fists by my side. 'Please understand, Liam, I love you. I'm not trying to hurt you.'

I try to place my hands on his shoulders, but he recoils and jerks away. His reactions hurt and I'm crying again, but the tears are tears of hope as much as they are tears of pain. He'll come around, in time.

This is not what I had in mind for our first dinner together, but we can work through it.

I know we can.

Chapter Thirteen

I sit, still strapped to the chair at the dining room table. My limbs are forced straight at an uncomfortable, unnatural angle, flush to the legs of the chair. The binds holding my wrists behind my back are tunnelling their way further into my skin, leaving it itchy and stinging with every movement.

She's crying again, but I don't feel pity anymore. I can't feel anything towards her except utter confusion. I have no idea why she is doing any of this to me. She's pottering around the room, shuffling around my chair and dragging her feet. She's tidying, I think, or at least appearing to be. Part of me is in absolute awe of her. I'm baffled, confused. I'm terrified. She speaks at me, looking right through my face, conversing with the wall behind me, tears overrunning the lip of her eyes. The rag presses against the back of my mouth and I plead with my eyes for her to remove it. I wish she'd just take it out, so I'm not on the verge of gagging. I just want to breathe.

'I won't be long, Liam. I hate mess, you see.'

This is insane. I grunt to get her attention, and she kneels down beside me. Her fingers linger across my jawline, skimming across my jugular and brushing over the fabric protruding from my mouth.

'I'll take it out. But if you shout or yell, I'll have to put it back. Or worse. Do you understand, Liam?' Her fingers trace the fabric, toying with it. The pleading eyes are not going to cut it.

I nod. I do understand. She pulls the rag from my throat, and I breathe deeply, thankful that the urge to vomit has left me for the time being.

'It's Noah,' I mumble. I let it escape under my breath before I can think of any logical reason to stop it. She turns on her heels to face me.

'What did you just say?'

I swallow, conscious of the phlegm struggling to get down my dry, hoarse throat.

'It's Noah. My name,' I repeat to her.

She stops tidying for a second, leaning on the table and turning square to face me.

'I don't need to explain this again, Liam,' she says, folding her arms and watching for my next words. Her eyes are intense and have locked onto mine. I'm afraid to look away in case she lashes out or strikes at me again.

I open my mouth to retaliate, but nothing comes - I don't feel like I have any words left. I have no idea what to say to this woman, what to say to her to rationalise with her. I try speaking up, but she cuts me off again. She's beyond reasoning with.

'What's in a name, anyway? It's a funny thing if you really think about it. Your name is only Noah because the two individuals that conceived you decided that they liked it more than the other little boy names that had been suggested to them.' She's talking to the room in general, I think. She doesn't look at me but continues fumbling with plates still full of food, pushing things around the table. She doesn't want any answers - this is not a conversation but more a monologue, a personal exploration of her thoughts.

'Even more ridiculously, they thought you *looked* like a Noah. What does that even mean? What does a *Noah* look like? We love labelling things, as a species. We can't leave anything unnamed. We're obsessed with assigning everything an identity. Anyway, I digress. What I'm trying to say is, I don't like the name Noah. I don't think it suits your face; I don't think it suits your personality or the way you talk or sound or stand. But I do like the name Liam. It sounds good. It sounds right alongside my name. I am sorry if you don't like it, but you'll just have to get used to it.' She finishes her lecture, still cleaning around me.

This is utterly insane. Try as I might, I can't make sense of what is happening, of how I ended up in this situation. One decision. One stupid decision to see if this woman needed my help and that stupid decision has landed me here. I'm not even sure where here is. A heavy fog is laying over my brain, seeping into each groove and crease as I clamber with the desperation to solve this bizarre puzzle, like my mind is wrapped in layers of impenetrable cling-film and no information can get either in or out.

'Noah is my name,' I say again over the clutter of her cleaning.

She turns to face me, swiping a knife from the table as she does. Her face is porcelain smooth and eerily calm, not a single line or wrinkle to give away what she's feeling inside. Her eyes hold onto their previous intensity.

'Don't make this harder than it needs to be, Liam.' The blade twists in her hand, grabbing the light from above my head and throwing it across my face - droplets of golden light, spattering over my cheeks. I can't take my eyes off each individual notch in the serrated steel. It's not the sharpest of blades, but I can't shift the idea of each tiny spike gripping into my skin like teeth, tearing at the flesh and pulling it apart like a zip down the front of a jacket. Do I let her feel like she's in control; is that the safer play or do I stick to my guns?

'I won't change my name for you,' I say, more confidently this time, far more confidently than I feel. 'It's Noah.' I hold my breath and wait for her reaction, for her outburst, but it doesn't come. Her eyebrows rise into an arch over the top of her steely blue eyes.

'It's not your decision to make,' she says as she flicks the knife over in her hand, so she's holding the handle in her palm. The blade runs up against her forearm, pushing into her pale skin but not penetrating the flesh. Her movements are nimble and effortless as she continues to mock me. Her blue irises lock onto my eyes again as her eyebrows lift. 'It was never your decision, don't you see?'

Her hand flies out past my face with absolutely no warning. The blade glints past my eye, a warning shot perhaps, and the blunt handle of the knife slams into the side of my head, ricocheting from my temple. She gives me no time to move, to tilt my head. Extreme pain explodes behind my eyes, erupting over my scalp and smouldering in my ears. I could vomit.

'What's your name?'

My eyes peel open against the pain dotting my vision like burning embers. She's towering over me, the knife hanging by her side.

'Noah,' I swallow, squinting through the flashing aura that threatens to take over my vision and the growing nausea in the pit of my stomach. My head lulls to the side, the weight of it swinging and lolloping against my chest. I blink hard as she brings the knife up again and slams it into the other temple in a quick, sharp movement, the handle bouncing off the side of my head. I bellow in agony. I've never felt pain like it, flooding over my head and rushing down my face and neck. The burning heat gathers behind my eyes and seeps all the way down my spine, coiling between each vertebra. Her talon-like fingers ram into my shoulders, clenching the feeble joints like a vice. She leans down beside me, her face inches away from my ear. Her breath is hot and brushes my neck as she speaks. It's so warm it's almost wet.

'What is your name?' She asks the question calmly, her humid breath licking my throat. She doesn't raise her voice, but she holds the knife in front of me, taunting me with it, reminding me that she can use it whenever she likes.

'Don't keep me waiting.'

I can't answer her; I'm too stubborn. My lips seal together in protest against this madness. I can't give up my name, my identity - I know that might become a slippery slope. My eyes are heavy; my eyelids soldered together with the pain and fire that's burning behind them.

She slams the knife back on the table, just a matter of feet away from me. A tiny lattice of light trickles in through my lashes, allowing me to watch her as she clears the table. I watch her through the tiny slit between the lids of my eyeballs, performing such mundane tasks as if the past few minutes never happened. As if none of this has happened at all. As if this is all completely normal to her. I watch her as I drift in and out of consciousness again. She collects cutlery, clears the plates, and sweeps crumbs of food into her palms to transport to the kitchen. As if it's all completely normal.

She grabs herself another glass of wine on her way back in and takes her seat at the table. The wine swills around the glass, clinging to the smooth, concave surface as it brushes just a little too close to each edge. She takes a sip and watches me as I drift off.

***

I hurt. Everything and everywhere hurts. My head hurts, my wrists hurt and now my face hurts, pain tingling and stinging across every inch of my body. My mind wanders when I let it, but I need to keep it together. It wanders to the corners of her mind, picturing what it is that she's got planned for me, what it is that she wants. The concern grows harder to control the longer I'm stuck here, and I'm aware that the longer I'm here, the harder it will be to get out.

I sit alone, tethered to a dining room chair, staring at a plate of diced up food. My stomach twinges with a pang of hunger, reminders of normal bodily functions that I'd all but forgotten about. I'm not touching what she's given me; I couldn't if I wanted to. The damp cloth has found its way back into my mouth, pressing into my throat and drying out my tongue. Even if I could eat anything she's left, I've decided I can't risk it. Ever. I can't chance it, no matter how good, how appetising it looks, or how unfathomably hungry I get, I cannot touch that food. Even when the salivating gets too much, and the cramps in my stomach render me useless, I cannot chance it. I can't trust her, even for a second. I can see the poison glistening from the potatoes, laced between the vegetables, dancing, tempting me to give in and eat. Go on, just one bite. Maybe it's a good thing the rag is still lodged in my throat. I am scared, I think. It's hard to process this, to rationalise what's swimming through my mind, to get a handle on what's happening, how to cope. It's all so surreal. My head is spinning; my mind is sloshing about between my ears.

My feet and arms are slowly going numb from the strain of being forced in the same position for hours on end. My joints and muscles are strained and fatigued. I don't know where she's gone, but I'm not calling her back. I can't. I don't want to risk her attacking me or force feeding me. I can just about hear her shuffling about. Maybe she's in the kitchen. I try to identify the sound. I try to work out what she's doing.

I'm strangely calm considering the situation I've found myself in. My mind has become detached from the situation. Maybe it's a coping mechanism. Any second now, any minute, she'll realise what she's done, snap out of it and let me go. Surely.

She's in the kitchen, whistling. Whistling as if she is happy, as if nothing about this is out of the ordinary. Whistling as if she's not got a care in the world.

Does she honestly think that she loves me - this woman that I've seen in the same coffee shop at the same time every day for the past few months? Sipping the same coffee, staring at the same table, out of the same window. The same woman that I've never, until today, held a full conversation with. I'd never even held eye contact with her. How was I to know that this was what was going through her mind?

God, if only I had known.

Chapter Fourteen

I'll make him wait a little longer; I'll play hard to get. We've got all the time in the world to spend together. A little space will probably do him good.

I swill the wine around in its glass, watching it stick to the sides and slide off the curved edges, leaving a shiny slug-like trail behind it. I hoist myself up onto the work surface, my feet dangling off the edges like a small child. He must be hungry now. He must, at least, be thirsty. Staying in here is just teasing him, dragging out the silence and leaving him to his own thoughts and the echoes they make in his mind. He'll come round to my way of thinking, eventually. He'll soon see what I see. I'll leave him no choice.

I throw the last few mouthfuls of wine down my neck. The rich alcohol burns as it hits and slides down the back of my throat. The glass sets down with a clink as I jump off the kitchen side.

Next to the glass is the new set of cooking knives I bought specifically for making our meals together. Six knives, six blades with smart, matte black handles all nestled snugly in order in their matching black wooden block. They're very uniform—very official looking. I remove one, a meat cleaver, unsheathing it from the block with a barely audible swish, revealing the impeccable silver blade in slow motion. I trace my hand just millimetres away from its sharp edge, the power rolling through my fingertips like electricity. The power of it, the potential damage it could cause, makes my mouth water. It takes all of my will power not to grab the blade, just to prove to myself that it's real, that this is all real. I stop myself from curling my fingers around the fresh knife-edge and watching it bite at my flesh with ease. Red gushing to the surface, trickling at first and then flowing more freely over the silver blade, intertwining through my fingers and meandering over the back of my hand. Blood pooling on the kitchen side, the scent of iron rising beautifully to the surface, red lace tracing its way over my hands.

I grip the handle of the knife and walk calmly back through to the living room. He's still sitting there, motionless. Not that I've given him much choice. I don't know why part of me is surprised to find him still sitting there. I sit opposite him and slide the knife out in front of me, making sure to catch his eye. My fingers linger on its handle, dancing across the blade, my gaze never breaking from his.

'You need to eat,' I order.

He holds my stare but doesn't respond, of course. The rag is still there, still filling his mouth. A white thread has unravelled from the fabric and hangs down the side of his chin, making him look like some kind of ventriloquist doll. I lean across the table and tug at the edge of the damp cloth, pulling it from between his teeth. An ungainly snort escapes from between his teeth.

'I'm so glad you've decided to stay, Liam. I guess I should have known better,' I say, dabbing at the corners of his mouth with the rag. 'I was so worried you'd leave me.'

He still doesn't respond, despite now being able to. I don't mind, just yet. I sit back in my chair, crossing my legs at the knee. He's just a toy to me, at this stage, a toy that I'm happy to flit between my paw-like hands, teasing and caressing and tormenting. He'll break eventually.

'Now, we can do this the easy way, or we can do it the hard way. It really is all down to you, Liam.'

His eyes have slipped from mine to the blade. They're looking a little haggard, exhausted, despite the amount of sleep he's had. I arch my back across the table, leaning my body-weight on one arm and take his face under his chin, forcing him to meet my stare.

'I've got nothing but your best interests at heart, Liam. I care about you deeply, and I want nothing more than for you to respond to me.' Each word fills my mouth like a glass ball, over pronounced and strong. I mean every word I say.

'That's not my name,' he whispers.

'Sorry, I didn't quite catch that.' I'm not letting this go, not this time.

That's not my name,' he repeats slightly louder, his head still tilted towards the table. He won't even look me in the eye.

'Is that really all you've got to say to me? We've talked about this, Liam - it's for the best.'

I mean it. I do care about him. Deeply. It hurts beyond words to see him brush away my affection so flippantly. I bring the fork back up to his mouth. He turns his head away again, refusing my kindness for the second time. I really can't condone his ungratefulness.

My right hand crawls across the table, making its way back to the knife. My fingers are back on the matte black handle, caressing the textured plastic. My fingertips dance across the handle, tapping the blade lightly and I watch in amusement as his eyes follow my every move.

'Just eat. Please,' I say, moving my hand seductively over the cleaver, exaggerating the movements for him to see, for him to understand the predicament he's put me in.

Again he turns his head in refusal. I don't want to have to keep threatening him, but his audacity leaves me no choice. I grab the knife from the table and bring it up over my shoulder. The blade flies effortlessly in my hand, splitting the air in two in front of Liam's face as I thrust it into the polished wood of the table. The knife is wedged in a good centimetre, maybe two in the mahogany. The speed and power of it meeting the table makes a comical sound as the metal briefly wobbles. He throws his head back to avoid the plummeting blade, his eyes so wide the skin threatens to split. I'm impressed he didn't make a sound, but his face gives away all I need to know.

'Will you listen to me now?' I scream, the sheer volume sharp in my throat, spit flinging from my lips into his face. He's terrified, I can see it. But still, he says nothing.

'God, I'm—I'm so sorry. Liam, please don't make me do that again.'

I hold out the food for him and wait. I can wait all evening if I have to. This time he leans in to take it off the fork. He anxiously accepts the food between his teeth, and I watch as he chews and swallows. The torment is visible in his eyes, but this is for the best. He'll see that soon.

'There, that's not so hard, is it? You'd think I was asking you to cut off your own arm.'

I try to talk to him some more as I slide another bite onto the fork, but he insists on sitting in silence. The next forkful hovers in front of his face. He swallows his pride and accepts the food, though his face is still full of trepidation and anxiety. It hurts me to see him so afraid of me, but if that's what it's going to take to get him to trust me and do as I say, then I suppose we'll just have to cope with it. He is taking the food more willingly now, chewing and swallowing in silence as I continue to talk.

'You know, I've watched you for a long time, Liam. I still remember the first day I saw you.' I pause, waiting for a reply that I'm almost certain won't materialise. His eyes flick up to mine for a brief second but are back down at the table in no time.

'That's fine, I don't need you to reply right now,' I say across the table, lifting the fork up to his mouth again.

'Sorry, where was I? So, I'd stumbled across that little coffee shop in my break at work, ordered a latte and sat in what would soon become my regular seat. I thought nothing more of it and sat by the window, basking in the late morning sunshine. I love sitting by the window, you see. Natural light is good for the soul. Anyway, I sat there, drinking and minding my own business, checking my phone and waiting for my break to end when the door to the coffee shop swung open and you walked in. You were wearing smart, pressed navy blue chinos, a white shirt, and brown leather shoes. You were unbelievably beautiful against the mediocre setting of the café. Your eyes glistened in the sun, and your hair was neatly swept back off your face. You were perfect. I fell for you the second I saw you. And the second I saw you; I knew I needed to have you.' The plate is gradually clearing as he accepts the food, still not replying but not arguing either.

'I've watched you in that café every day since. I watched you come in, watched you order, watched you drink your coffee and watched you leave to go back to your office. And I was perfectly happy to watch and admire you from afar until that day last week when you turned up at *our* café with another woman. I couldn't bear it, Liam. I couldn't bear to see you with another woman. I couldn't stomach the way you looked at each other, full of affection and excitement. The way you touched her face and swept her hair out of her eyes. I was desperate for that woman to be me. I wanted so much for you to look at me that way, to place your hand delicately on my face and blush when our hands accidentally touched on the table. I felt sick to see you with her. And it was then that I decided I couldn't just let her have you without a fight. I needed to show you how much I care for you. She might think you're handsome or interesting or whatever shallow thing it is she sees in you, but I *love* you Liam, and I couldn't let her get in the way of that. That's why I brought you here, to show you what you mean to me. To show you how much I want to take care of you. Do you understand?'

I wait for his response, but of course, it never arrives. I stare at him for a minute or two. He's looking down at the remnants on his plate, presumably waiting for me to wait on him some more.

'I don't think so,' I say, sliding the cutlery together at the bottom of the plate. 'I think we're done for now.' I stand up with the plate and walk it through to the kitchen. If he wants to act like a petulant child, then I'm happy to treat him as such.

I dump the whole plate, food and all, into the sink, grab a cloth and walk back over to the table. I kneel beside him and wipe gently at his face, removing the stray crumbs from the corners of his lips. He flinches at first, but gives in and lets me clean his face. I think he's finally learning.

'There, that wasn't so bad.' I lay the cloth on the table and lean in towards his face. I kiss him, laying my lips gently on his, though he doesn't reciprocate the gesture. My mouth presses more firmly against his as I push my tongue between his teeth, my tongue brushing against his tongue, hand resting on his thigh. He's statuesque, his eyes remaining cold and unflinching. My face moves against his, and I try with all my energy to be passionate, to evoke some kind of reaction from him. But I get nothing. He doesn't move an inch. I press my lips gently on his forehead, pulling my face away from his.

'You'll love me eventually,' I hiss, shoving the rag back into his mouth.

I have planned for this day meticulously. Every day I've lived so far has just been leading up to this one moment; I have thought of every eventuality, have enacted every possible conversation, argument, and small talk chat in my head. But nothing I've prepared or thought about has equipped me to deal with the silence that fills my home.

I walk back into the living room and start untying the ropes at Liam's ankles. He flicks his gaze down towards me. I can see it, the unmistakable glint of hope in his eyes. The hope that I'm letting him go, setting him free. The hope fills his eyes like an beacon. I almost laugh in his face at his naivety. I leave his hands cuffed and drag him out of the chair. He's wobbly on his feet, unsteady like a newborn animal. I can almost hear the pins and needles crackling through his limbs like burning embers. His knees threaten to cave under the weight of his body, and he stumbles over his feet in an attempt to remain upright. I catch him by the shoulders, stopping him from falling back into the chair and pull him into me. My arms wrap around his torso as I yank his head down closer to mine.

'Don't flinch, don't try to run. I've got that knife in my hand—do not make me use it.' I push the handle of the knife against his rib cage, just a gentle reminder. 'Don't force me to do something neither of us wants.'

I kiss him again, pressing my mouth against his cold, stern lips. I lead him into the bathroom, one hand in the small of his back and the other holding the blade just a few inches from his throat.

'Don't try anything,' I whisper into his ear, pushing him through the door and into the gleaming white room. The lock crunches closed as I fasten Liam's cuffs to the pole above the sink.

'I'll give you a few minutes to get yourself ready,' I say, leaving the door open and walking backwards to sit on the bed. I can see him clearly through the door from where I sit. I watch him, awkwardly looking around our bathroom for the first time.

Liam

I spread my hand on the cool tiled sink, stretching my fingers out across the surface. The things organised on the worktop - they're meant for me. They're ordered meticulously and lined up parallel to the sink on top of the immaculately polished white surface. She bought them for me: the shampoo, the toothbrush, the dressing gown hanging on the back of the door with that unmistakable new fabric smell. The razor, the comb, the cologne. The cologne I've worn every day for as long as I can remember.

Even in here I don't have any privacy, not a second to calculate or process what's going on. I can feel her eyes on me, studying me. She's sat on the bed, her hands resting on her lap, just watching, always watching. Her eyes are boring into me, judging my every movement. Her hand is resting on the knife, just in my line of sight, her fingers pirouetting over the blade.

The bathroom is small; I can just about touch each wall from where I stand, my arm twisting awkwardly against the cuffs. I turn my head to the back wall to hide my embarrassment and shunt my body over to the toilet. Humiliation rises in my stomach like vomit. The whole experience is degrading to a level that I never thought I'd experience. I've known this woman for a matter of hours, and she's reduced me to this. I'm dehumanized. Disgraced. I don't turn to see, but I can feel her still staring at me, even now.

'Oh, I'd love to give you some privacy, but you know I can't risk that,' she says in her falsely happy, lyrical tone. I remain facing away from her, but even so, I can tell she's basking in this, enjoying the power she has over me.

My back is still turned. I steal a few breaths facing the wall, the smallest amount of solitude I've managed to scrape together since arriving here. I flick my eyes around the room once more in search of a clock, some small reminder of normality. Time feels dangerously fluid now, running through my fingers, spilling onto the floor. I don't recall seeing any clocks in the whole apartment.

She's still sat there, waiting for me. She wears a thin smile that doesn't translate to her eyes. I don't know what she wants me to say. I don't know what she actually wants from me at all. Everything is lined up perfectly by the sink - regimented and standing to attention. The bathroom is clinically clean, not a single spot of damp or dust clinging to the grouting in between the tiles. It's all perfectly white, as if it were only finished days ago. The acrid scent of bleach is everywhere. She's crossed her legs at the knee, her arms behind her supporting her torso.

I flick open the lid to the toothpaste with my free hand, managing to squeeze some of the white and blue paste onto the new toothbrush currently resting in between the electric shaver and the shampoo. I turn the tap, wet the brush and clean my teeth. I shoot a glance over to see her still sitting, like a mother watching their child gain their independence. I'm a grown man, shackled to a pipe in a bathroom, being inspected before bed. I'm learning a new routine that I don't want to be a part of.

I throw the toothbrush down on the side and drag my hand across my face. The brush falls wherever it wants to fall, knocking other things out of line, a small disturbance of the current order. I signal to Sarah that I'm finished.

She peels herself off the bed and makes her way over. Her slender fingers push the toothbrush back into its empty space nestled between the shaver and the shampoo. The knife is still in her hand. The blade catches the bathroom light and throws a kaleidoscope of glistening triangles around the room. I'm unshackled and unchained, but I don't run. I can't bring myself to chance it whilst she's got that knife so close to my face; I have no doubt that she'd use it now.

She walks me through to the bedroom pushing me into a chair by the wardrobe and begins to tie me back to the heavy wooden frame. Her breathing is deep and strong, accented by the swish of the rope twisting in swathes between my ankles and the polished wooden chair legs. The movements swoop and swirl in the air by my feet. The fibres in the rope make a zipping sound as she tugs at them, pinching my skin and yanking my legs against the wood. It's tied uncomfortably tight, but I know it will go numb soon enough.

She runs her hands seductively up my thighs, edging dangerously close to my groin. There's a playful glint in her eye, another flash of power. I let her do it; there's nothing I can logically do to contest it. I'm in no position to push her away, and there's no use saying anything. My hands are already behind me, pulling my torso rigid to the back of the chair. She sweeps her hands up between my legs and brushes them over to my thighs. She pushes into my hips and swings a leg up over my lap. She's straddling me, her back arched and forcing her chest towards my face. Her body rocks against my lap and I can just about make out her whispering between gentle purrs of enjoyment. My breath catches in my throat as she pecks my neck, her tiny kisses growing in strength as they travel down my throat, closer to my torso. It takes every ounce of willpower not to lean into her kisses, to not reciprocate her passion. I almost let it take over me.

She slides her hands up my torso, clasping them around the back of my head and forces my neck up towards her face. She leans in to kiss me again, her warm, soft lips suddenly feeling alien against my mouth. I freeze up as soon as she makes contact, my whole body turning rigid.

'This is getting silly,' she says as she shoves her hand into my shoulder to push herself away. Despite my current predicament, I find myself feeling sorry for her, in a warped way. She looks rejected. She sounds rejected. I think she's been here before, perhaps. In love, or convinced that she's in love with someone, and them having absolutely no feeling for her whatsoever. In normal circumstances, I might have considered kissing her back. But with every touch of her lips, I feel more and more sick.

'When will you give in, Liam? When will you love me?' She's desperate for an answer. I try not to give one, but my mouth answers before my brain can tell it otherwise.

'I can't love you. I couldn't possibly love you.' She moves away from me, dejected, and for once since my arriving here she doesn't answer me. 'Why don't you just–let me go? Untie me, and we can talk about this properly.' It's a semi-serious offer.

'I'm not stupid, Liam.' She turns to stare at me, holding my gaze like an animal does their prey.

'It's Noah,' I mumble again, defeated. She ignores the mention of my real name and moves closer towards me.

'Just kiss me back.' She's pleading now, begging for me to give in. It's embarrassing to watch her, actually. She's not just asking me anymore, she's literally begging on her hands and knees, imploring me to reciprocate her feelings. I try to turn my head away, but she grabs my face in her hand and forces it back into her line of sight. 'Just love me, Liam. Just one kiss, please?'

'I can't, Sarah. You're obviously going through something. What your boyfriend did to you–it's clearly affected you.'

I watch her face for some kind of reaction; it's almost like she's forgotten. Almost as if she has misplaced the memories from earlier and forgotten any conversation we had about her boyfriend and the abuse and the hitting and the crying.

The room explodes with maniacal laughter. She's cackling hysterically, a raw, unnerving sound on the verge of mental instability. She's still sitting on my lap, her head thrown back and her mouth hanging wide. Her laugh fills every corner of the bedroom, ricocheting off the walls as her back arches and her chest heaves. She slows herself down, breathing deeply, steadying herself and gripping onto my shoulder. She takes a deep, deliberate breath.

'You actually still think I was telling you the truth? You believed me? You believed that I'd been abused. You really think I'd let some man get the better of me? You've got a lot to learn.'

She kisses me again, swinging her legs off my lap and placing her hand on my shoulder. She gives it a squeeze, an oddly endearing gesture for such an odd situation. She places a blanket over my lap and rests the knife down on the bedside cabinet beside her.

'I'm a terribly light sleeper, I'm afraid, so probably best not to try anything stupid.'

She walks over to the bedroom door and closes it. The door looks reinforced. It's made of a heavy material that shunts closed as she pushes it. Two locks adorn the door; one traditional that she slides the key into and twists and the other looks similar to the locks on the doors back at the office with a complicated looking keypad. She thumbs in a combination too far away for me to identify and walks back over to the bed, placing the key from the first lock into the pocket of her pyjamas. She slides into bed, not breaking eye contact with me the entire time and grabs the knife to place under her pillow. Her body sinks into the mattress, and she rests on her elbows, looking directly at me.

'This isn't how I imagined this would turn out, you know, having you move in? I just expected you to be happy.'

'Expected me to be happy?' The words flood from my mouth. 'What is wrong with you? How could you possibly think that?'

'Liam, I understand that this might take time. That's okay; I have nothing but time,' she replies, unfazed. A playful grin teases the corners of her lips. She looks amused that I'm kicking up such a fuss, that I'm acting like such a child. That I deserve to be ignored for a few hours to have a good hard think about what I've done.

'Can you hear yourself, Sarah? Can you hear what you're saying? Let me go! This is ridiculous!' My voice builds in a crescendo as I scream. Spit gathers at the corners of my mouth and flies across the room.

'No one can you hear, Liam. I know what you're trying to do and no one is coming for you. I made sure of it. Now be quiet,' she says, shoving the old rag back into my mouth.

'Goodnight, Liam.'

My mind is empty. All rational thoughts and reactions to the events of the past 12 hours seem to have left me, seem to have slipped through my conscience like grains of sand through a sieve. I can't muster up the energy to respond to her, even to groan through the spit-soaked cloth. She leaves the bedside lamp on, the blade now nestled under the pillow and me firmly shackled to a chair with a blanket thrown over my lap.

It's only as I sit here in the dark that I realise I've not thought about her at all. About Ella, the girl that Sarah saw me with. She is actually my on-off girlfriend of the past couple of months, but it's never developed into anything other than a playful fling. Up until now, I'd not even thought about her.

***

His eyes have finally dropped.

I forced myself to stay awake to make sure he nodded off first.

He tried to fool me a few times, I think, closing his eyes against the warm, orange glow of the lamp, groaning soft, fake snores under his breath. But you can tell when someone has genuinely fallen. You can tell when their mind has slipped from their consciousness and the weight of the day all piles into their limbs, tugging at their body like an abandoned ragdoll.

I watched as he finally admitted defeat against the day. His head dropped like deadweight, flopping forwards in front of him. His shoulders sagged; his breathing deepened, swelling his chest rhythmically. I stared at him for a long while.

His face is even more beautiful in this light, warm and rich. I watch him as he finally relaxes and breathes, as his chest and back rise up like a hot air balloon and fall back down, deflating with every exhalation. It's therapeutic to witness - my new favourite spectator sport. I could get used to staring at him every night.

I'm exhausted now though. He did take a good couple of hours or so to finally drop off, and I couldn't bring myself to sleep whilst he was still awake. I wrap my fingers around the handle of the blade, stroking the cool plastic surface to remind myself that it's there, there for me to use if need be. The blade is icy cool under my pillow, vibrating with power and potential.

His breathing gets deeper and deeper, until it becomes a faint rumble, almost a snore. My eyes are stinging and sore from the exhaustion. I can feel my breathing getting heavier, getting deeper and deeper alongside his. I sink into the mattress as my limbs fill with lead and my fingers unfurl around the knife as they finally relax. I sink into the white noise, drift off and leave my bedroom behind.

I'm in a meadow.

Not one that I've ever seen or been in before. I've probably borrowed the image from an advert or someone else's memory, a book in a doctor's waiting room, perhaps. I can see my mother, stood to the right of me. And my grandmother knelt on the floor beside her. They're pandering over someone, though I'm not sure whom. I'm stood on my own, watching them. They're always fussing over someone else—always paying attention to something other than me. I think they know I'm here, but they're ignoring me.

My hands feel sticky, maybe slightly wet, sweaty perhaps. Initially, I think it's due to the heat, but when I look down, I know it's something different entirely. My hands are dripping. They're shiny with a dark, red liquid, so opaque I can't see my flesh underneath. It's blood. I pad my chest, run my hands over my torso and my limbs and my face, through my hair, over my knees and my elbows and stomach. It's not mine. The blood isn't mine. I've streaked it all over my body, all over my clothes, but it's not mine.

I look down at my feet. The red is trailed through the grass, smeared and dragged through the individual blades, staining the green a horrific, dark, clotted red. It leads away from me, drawing a line towards my mother.

A whistle of quivering breath escapes my lips, trembling as my whole body shakes with nerves. I'm conscious of everything now, every blade of grass that ripples in the breeze, every drop of thick, gluey blood that tumbles off the end of my fingertips. What's happened here?

I need to know. I need to find out. But my feet won't move from this spot. They're welded to the floor, cemented to the earth underneath my feet.

Maybe it's not as bad as it looks. Maybe it's a joke or a misunderstanding. Maybe there's more to this story that I'm not privy to.

I taste tin on my lips—the tang of iron against my tongue. My mother's hand is resting on her mother's shoulder, consoling her, I think. I can almost hear her saying everything will be just fine, but her lips don't move.

I stagger a few steps forward towards the two of them, heaving my leaden feet as if I were shackled to the ground. The closer I get, the more I can hear. I still can't see anything, but I can hear my grandmother crying. Old sobs, croaky, choking tears, peppered with pain and age. She's kneeling beside something, maybe someone. Not someone I recognise. I take another step closer, trembling as I do.

My mother whips round to face me, holding her hand out in front of her.

'Stay there, Emily! Don't move!'

Her voice freezes me to the spot. I stand, rigid, eyes wide and staring over at my mother.

'Mum--?'

'No, Emily!' She bellows at me, screaming at me to stay put.

I listen. I tilt my head to try to see more from where I'm stood. My grandmother looks like she is stroking something. She's running her hands through something's fur or through its hair, I can't really tell.

'Grandma—what are you doing?'

I walk closer, ignoring the persistent yells of my mother, ignoring her waving hands and frantic eyes. I need to see what it is.

I'm just a few feet away now. Whatever it is is being completely shielded by my Grandmother's torso. It's blocked from my vision.

153

'Please, Grandma. What is it? What are you doing? What are you hiding?'

She spins up onto her feet, much quicker than I ever remember her being able to before. She's guarding whatever she is hiding, shielding it from me, and protecting it from me.

My eyes flick down to her feet. I catch a glimpse of something between her shoes, laced between the long blades of grass. The fleshy pink tones of young skin look so delicate amongst the greenery. Little fingers on little hands, nestled amongst the meadow. Pale fingers weaving in and out of the grass, planted between the blades. They're not moving, the fingers. Nor the hand, nor the arm that the hand belongs to.

My mother is crying silent tears. The more I watch and stand and stare, the more I panic, and the more my heart beats in my chest.

A tear rolls off my chin, hitting my white shirt and staining it an off-pink colour. I did something terrible, but I can't remember what. But I know that I'm just inches away from it. And I can feel the reality of it tugging at my chest.

'Grandma?' I ask her, calling her name as I walk closer. With every step, she seems to get further away, until the scene rushes up on me all at once.

I see it then, crumpled up on the floor, lifeless and still and beautiful. The boy's body deflated and bloody, sprawled amongst the dirt. His eyes are open and staring at me, but not moving. There's no life in them anymore.

I look up at my mother, desperate for her to say something that will make sense of this mess. She doesn't speak. She just continues to stare at the boy.

'You did this,' my Grandmother says. 'This was your fault. You did this.' She doesn't sound angry or scared, just disappointed, numb maybe.

She isn't crying. I'm not sure that she recognises the boy. I'm not sure my mother does either.

I can't have done this. I don't even know whom this little boy is, where he came from. I couldn't even tell you his name. I edge a few steps closer until I can read the emotion on his face. He looks calm, restful. Frozen in time, but not scared or frightened. There's a bright, shiny splash of yellow just by his neck—sticking out above the collar of his shirt. I can't quite make out what it is at first, but I soon recognise it. It's my father's—the yellow thing. I must have swiped it from the shed on the way out of the house. I must have snuck it out in my jacket pocket again. I always stick things in my pockets that aren't mine, to see if I can steal them without being noticed. It's an innocent thing. I like to push the boundaries. That boy must have annoyed me, I imagine.

The yellow thing is the handle of an old screwdriver. An old screwdriver that is protruding from the boy's neck, soaked in his blood and undoubtedly covered in my fingerprints.

Chapter Fifteen

Liam.

I did drift off for a while. I can't see any clocks about so I don't know what the time is or how long I was out for. Despite the glow of the lamp, I can see that it is still dark outside–maybe the early hours of the morning? It's that strange time of night where the darkness takes on a blue tinge, and the mist scatters across the sky. My mind is groggy, full of cotton wool and fog. I'm slightly nauseous from exhaustion. Nerves and anxiety have been steadily building in my chest since I got here. It sits there, now, next to my heart, a small ball of worry growing and growing, taking on more layers of worry and concern, threatening to spiral out of control if I pay too close attention to it.

Sarah is out cold as far as I can tell. Her head has sunk deep into the pillows, hiding her face in soft mounds of white. Her face looks peaceful, but her hand rests on the knife under her head. She's still got hold of it, still showing me that she's not afraid to use it, to plunge it into my chest without a minutes notice. Every now and then, her feet judder and kick out of the covers as if she is in the middle of a deep dream, slipping deeper into her sleep. The bed looks incredibly comfortable and, the more the pain and discomfort grows in my legs, the more comfortable it looks. My back is in agony, my neck is throbbing, and sharp shooting pains have started to dart up my legs in clusters. She does look so comfortable in that bed. There's no way I'm going to be getting any more sleep sat to attention, strapped to this chair.

I need to try to keep my mind busy, to make sense of this place and familiarise myself with my surroundings. It's like a game. Study the room and try to commit it all to memory. Every detail. Every crease in the curtains, every notch in the wall, every ridge in the bed-sheets. I'll test myself later.

The bed is almost perfectly in the centre of the room, the curved back of the headboard leaning into the far wall. Each side of the bed has its own small wooden table with a white lamp and a few, nondescript novels shoved in the compartment underneath. I can't see what the novels are - the odd thriller or crime paperback, perhaps. The wardrobes are built in—they're the sliding kind with the mirrored doors, not a single fingerprint floating across the surface. The curtains are a blush colour, though that could be the light of the lamp manipulating them. They look quite heavy, hanging and pooling at the bottom of the window in puddles of liquid satin, as if they're slightly too long.

There are images on the walls, similar to those that are in the living room. Images of unrealistically happy couples walking hand in hand through a forest, another of the same couple at dinner, and another of a few different people who are definitely different but look somewhat the same walking a dog in the park. The people feel real enough, but there's something disconcerting about their perfection. And Sarah doesn't seem to be in any of the images. She's not in a single picture that I've seen throughout the whole flat. It's like she doesn't exist, like she's the one always lurking behind the camera rather than cheerily wishing away her life in front of it. It's like the people in the pictures don't know who she is.

Every person in each image has a relatable quality, a memorable face; I've seen them somewhere before, but I just don't know where. They form part of a ghost of a memory or a strange imprint–not strong enough to put my finger on but strong enough for me to be sure that I know who they are. Somehow.

Everything in the room looks brand new. Even the carpet and the bed linen and the artwork and the polished glass doors of the sliding wardrobes. The carpet has stripes dragged through it from recent vacuuming, lines pulled through the ply. Every last inch looks like a show room in a modern new flat, devoid of character, impeccable. Perfect for a hotel but by no means homely. There's not a speck of dust anywhere. It's like sitting amongst the pages of a catalogue, in a vaguely familiar room that I've seen somewhere once before. Everything seems to have been placed there for a reason, purposefully placed to rest.

Sarah's breathing is shallow but relaxed. It whispers around the room, constantly reminding me that I'm not alone. My breath catches in my throat, and I struggle to remind myself that I am okay, for now. I can breathe; I'm alive. I am okay. I count in my head and touch my fingertips to the cool metal of the handcuffs, grounding my mind in reality and trying not to give in to the panic. My mouth is dry; each tiny taste bud is inflamed and desperate for water, bristling on the surface of my tongue. Tiny hands all around my mouth reaching and grabbing desperately for moisture. Swallowing is getting harder. My mouth is getting drier. I tug at the handcuffs, pulling my hands away from the rear of the chair and wince. They're secure, all right. The metal digs into my wrists, and I stifle a groan of pain. The ropes are just as tight around my ankles, grazing into my bare skin.

I almost wish I could fall back to sleep, but my body is so full of nerves that I know the slumber would be riddled with nightmares and jumps and starts. I try to bring my mind back round to rationality again as the panic threatens to suffocate me. Every nerve ending, every cell in my body is standing to attention.

I can't escape right now. I can't move; I can't free myself from this chair. I need to calm down and think this through. I can only just breathe. I'm struggling not to choke on my own breath. I catch myself fidgeting, my feet bouncing inches off the floor and eyes darting around the room. I struggle to keep it together, to hold my balance, like feet digging into tumbling gravel on a steep hill. I can't concentrate–I can't stop to think.

How on earth did I not realise she'd been watching me for weeks? Stalking me, following me, her eyes all over me every time I left my flat. She knows where I work, she knows where I live, and she knew how to fool me into feeling sorry for her and following her back here. She lured me into her trap. I don't know what makes me feel more uneasy–the fact that she's been following me for an undisclosed amount of time, or the fact that she is utterly convinced that she is in love with me and expects me to learn to love her back. It's beyond delirium.

And she drugged me. I know she drugged me.

Once she'd lured me in here to feel sorry for her–poor victimised her! She had me just where she wanted me. She tricked me into her living room, into her home, into her armchair. She slipped something into my tea, watched it dissolve and swirl on the surface of the liquid. Thinking back to it now I can taste it, roll it around on the surface of my tongue.

My eyes flit back to the bathroom door and all of the items lined up by the sink just behind it. She knew I was coming. She'd planned for this. Every item in there lined up, each perfectly parallel to the next. The men's shampoo, the men's shower gel, the razor, each with their own space. I'd assumed they belonged to her abusive ex-partner, but I can feel the truth of it all settling over me now. I can see the truth in every unopened toiletry. Everything in here has been bought for me. For me specifically. With me in mind. Everything is brand new; the seals freshly peeled away, waiting for me to arrive.

She's been following me, potentially for months–maybe longer. She knows how I take my coffee; she knows what I do for work. But I don't know how deep she's gone. If what she knows about me–or thinks she knows–is all superficial, if she's merely scraped across the surface. I don't know just how much she knows about my life, if she really knows anything of value at all. If she knows that my family, all but one estranged sibling, has passed away. If she knows that I live in this area on my own, in complete solitude. If she knows that I've hidden my emotions for years and have drowned my thoughts in my work, in a dreary office where no one really knows me past the name placard on my door. That there is no one here that cares for my well-being or cares for me in a way that would cause concern if I were to just not to turn up to work one day. No one will be worried about me. No one will even notice that I'm not there. I have no one. And if she knows that, then she chose me specifically.

***

The sun peeks through the new curtains. It's peering in now, seeping through the fabric and throwing highlights over the bed, casting thin shadows across Liam's face. He still sat in the same position, half awake, his head lolling to the side with the weight of exhaustion. It's nice to wake up with him by my side, even if that does mean he's outside the bed for now. It feels right. This is the beginning of the rest of our lives. Spending every minute possible together. I can't wait to know him like the back of my hand.

'Morning,' I say with a smile. I place my hand on his knee, and he jerks fully awake. He looks around sleepily, as if remembering or seeing this room for the first time.

He looks nervous. I don't think he's slept very well, strapped to that chair. It doesn't look like he's even tried to get some shut-eye. Heavy grey bags drag at the corners of his eyes, and his face is grey with fatigue and five o'clock shadow. He rolls his neck, the bones cracking in protest and he blinks against the daylight. I prop myself up on my elbow to see him better, tilting my head to the side.

'How did you sleep?'

'How do you think?' His voice is croaky and strained in his dry throat. He sounds shattered–not just tired but emotionally broken, his personality cracking and fraying at the edges. Deep red veins litter the whites of his eyes, crawling around his iris like branches of a macabre tree.

I'm growing impatient already. I just want us to have a normal relationship. I want him to let me love him, to let me in.

'I can make us coffee, if you want?'

He doesn't answer, but I assume he wants one anyway. I roll out of bed, careful to flash just enough of the blade in Liam's direction to remind him that it's still there, that I'm still in control of this. I think he could do with a few minutes to sit on his own, to let his new home and surroundings sink in in the daylight.

I stand by the door, slide in the key and enter the combination to disable the second lock. I leave him for a few minutes, securing the door from the outside, just to make sure. I'm not sure why I bother–he can't go anywhere. I'm nervous, leaving him to his own thoughts, but I know he'll come around eventually. He'll have no choice but to.

I walk gently to the kitchen, leaving him to sit alone once more.

I think I dreamt again last night, but I slept so well, so fully, that I can barely remember any of the details. It's irritating, at first, trying to remember something that doesn't want to be remembered, to scratch at something below that surface that just doesn't want to be uncovered. I give up eventually. Why worry about a dream or a sleeping memory when I have this new potential and energy in my life, right in front of me?

I make two cups of coffee and walk them back through to the bedroom. He's exactly how I left him—staring hollowly at the foot of the bed. I place the mugs down on the bedside table and start to unlock the cuffs that have held his hands behind his back for over 12 hours. It's risky to free his hands up, I know, but I need to start to show him that I can trust him. Besides, he can't hold a cup with his arms like that, and I don't want to belittle him by feeding him his drink.

The small key slips easily between the mechanism and the lock clicks open. Liam grunts as he pulls his shoulders around to the front of his body. He's hunched over now, arms stiff and jarring against his torso, stiffened and aching as a result of the 12 or so hours that they were held behind his back. I still have the blade close to my thigh so he can see it—so he knows it's not worth risking anything stupid, so he knows how serious I am about all of this. I bring his arms to his lap. The joints and muscles groan and creak as I loosen them. He looks noticeably more comfortable already. I do slide the cuff back over his free hand once they're both on his lap, but looser than before. I place the cup between his hands, enveloping his fingers around the warm earthenware mug and smile. He half offers a smile back.

'Thank you,' he says, staring at the steaming, brown liquid. I watch him as he sips the coffee, inhaling the fumes, running his fingers over the surface of the cup.

'Not a problem,' I say. 'I thought we'd stay in today, if that's okay with you? I feel like we've got so much learning to do—about each other, I mean.'

His eyes flick up from his lap and make contact with mine. At first, they say pain, torment, annoyance, confusion, but after a few breaths resignation washes over his irises.

'Sure, okay,' he says as he lets out a deep, long exhalation.

It's more than I can hope for, really. I'm thrilled he's open to talking today, to getting to know each other, to giving this a chance.

Liam

In the early hours of this morning, whilst staring out at the dusky night sky, I came to the conclusion that the only way I would be able to get out of this situation is to play Sarah at her own game.

I need to give her what she wants.

I need to make it look like I'm willing to learn to love her. Like I'm willing to learn to like it here, to live this way. It's not going to be easy, but I'm sure there won't be any other way. I've been thinking about it for hours now, racking my brain trying to work out the best way to go about it. It needs to be gradual; it needs to be wholly convincing. I can't wake up tomorrow morning and declare my love for her. She'll know I'm lying. She's many things, but she's clearly not stupid.

So I need to play the long game.

I need to make it look like I'm slowly coming round to the idea of this being my home. And it's not going to be easy.

I'm currently cuffed to a chair, trapped in a room with multiple locks on the door, staring out of a tiny gap in the curtains from a basement flat with bars on the windows. No one knows I'm here and no one cares. I have no one to rely on but myself, and I need to convince her, I need to trust that she'll fall for it.

'There you go,' she says, placing a mug of coffee between my hands and breaking into my internal conversation.

She left me to sit here alone whilst making the hot beverages in the kitchen, a perfectly normal, mundane thing to do for someone in the morning when you've just woken up. It's so surreal, doing such a normal thing but in such unusual circumstances. I don't think she's registered how extraordinary all of this is. She's treating this whole fiasco as entirely normal, not an inch out of the ordinary.

I stare down at the drink she's made me, and the thought that she may be drugging me invades my consciousness again. I imagine it, the poison, floating and swirling on top of the coffee, slipping down my throat and violating my bloodstream. The contaminated substance dripping through my veins and dragging my eyes shut against their will, rendering me motionless. I can almost smell it. I force my mouth open against my tightened tendons and take a sip, offering her a small smile and a nod of thanks.

I grit my teeth and muster the most sincere voice I can manage.

'Thank you.'

She seems to like it and beams at me, her hand back on my knee and her face full of energy and light.

'Not a problem,' she replies.

What a normal, uninteresting conversation. It's easy to forget that this woman is currently holding me prisoner in her bedroom. She's so casual and easy, I keep catching myself wondering if I'm overreacting, if this is more normal than I realise.

She starts to open up to me, and we talk. It's all awkward small talk at first. The weather, the price of the wallpaper and new bedspread in her room, the cost of bills to heat the flat nowadays, the state of public transport, really benign small talk wedged into such an odd situation. It's awkward and stunted, but it's a start. And I let it happen as naturally as I can. She likes to talk. She likes the sound of her own voice, I think. She doesn't seem to be too offended if I don't reply much beyond the odd word or two. I'm not sure she has the opportunity to have much conversation with anyone else.

'So where do your family live? Are they far away?' She's asking me questions now with her head placed on her hands, resting on her lap. Her face seems genuinely interested in what I have to say, but it's hard to tell the difference between legitimate intrigue or if, in reality, she's just collecting facts about me, stowing them away to use at a later date.

I shake my head. 'They're from the town across, just a couple of stops on the train,' I lie. 'I have a pretty good relationship with them, as relationships with family go.'

I watch her eyes as I fabricate my false family relationships for the first time. She seems to accept it without question and nods, shifting her head in her hands.

'What about yours?'

She nods in agreement. 'Not far from here, but I don't have a great relationship with them, to be honest. They don't like the way I am, so I don't tend to let them in. I haven't seen my mother in a few years; we never saw eye-to-eye. For all I know, she could think I'm dead.'

She ended the sentence abruptly, stifling the already awkward conversation, snuffing it out like you would a candle between your fingertips. She shuffles on the bed, clearly annoyed at herself for divulging too much too soon.

'I'll, erm—do you want some breakfast?'

I nod to relieve her from the tension and watch her as she leaves. This time she doesn't lock the door on her way out and leaves it open so I can see into the hallway. I can hear her fumbling and crashing around in the kitchen; our exchange has clearly upset her. There's a loud bang as a drawer is yanked open and thrown back into place, accented by the clang of cutlery sliding freely from one side of the drawer to the other.

I stare at my hands resting in my lap as she makes breakfast. The cuffs have cut into my wrists and burrowed deep, red rings all the way around, making my hands look almost detachable from the rest of my arm. A glance down to my feet confirms that my ankles haven't fared much better. The ropes have irritated and grazed my skin, burning their mark into the pale flesh at the bottom of my legs. The ties that bound me to this chair for countless hours have left me feeling like a mannequin, equipped with removable appendages and no voice or free will. If Sarah came back and tugged at my hands, I'm almost certain they'd come away from my forearms without much convincing.

A few minutes later she returns, carrying a plate of toast and more watery coffee. It's only when I see the food that I realise how hungry I am. The shame of last night's situation forced me to refuse the food for as long as possible. I couldn't bring myself to accept it until the very last minute. And it's only on seeing the two meagre slices of bread on the earthenware plate that I realise the pangs of hunger in my stomach. It also occurs to me how grateful I feel for the small amount of food, how she's made me feel I need to be grateful for the small break in her abuse. She hands me a slice, and I eat it in silence as she watches and eats her own.

'So,' she says, looking up from the plate. 'What is it you do for work exactly?'

'I'm in finance, account management, that sort of thing. I thought you already knew that?'

I couldn't help myself; the inflammatory comment snuck in before I had a chance to stop it. She raises an eyebrow and ignores the remark, returning to the awkward, first date style questioning.

So, what do you do for fun? What are your hobbies? Did you grow up here? What was the name of your first pet? What's your favourite colour? Blah blah blah.

It's draining, being drilled for answers that don't matter, answering questions that won't change anything. But I do feel like I'm getting to know her better, and the majority of my answers are truthful, which is as much a surprise to me as it is to her, I'm sure.

We keep talking. Small questions about things we like and dislike, shallow things, superficial things. Sarah makes the bed and dresses in front of me in-between her quizzing. One question, another item of clothing. A light-hearted attempt at a humorous remark that doesn't really land given that I'm still tied to a chair, another item of clothing. It goes on like this until she's fully dressed and she trots into the bathroom to apply makeup, brush her teeth, sort her hair, that sort of thing. Once she's finished, she comes back into the bedroom to briefly set me free. My knees are shaky and weaker than I thought they'd be.

I find myself shackled to the pipe above the sink again, shuffling around the small bathroom trying to clean myself up. She's leaning just inside the room watching me, her back arching against the doorframe. I finish brushing my teeth, and she leans over to dab stray toothpaste from the corners of my mouth. I pull my head back as her thumb hovers over my lips, tracing their outline, but she moves closer towards me and rests her fingertips briefly on my cheek. She leans in close, but I can't bring myself to allow it, not yet. I flinch away, turning my head to the floor.

'So what's the plan for today?' I ask, edging slightly further away from her hand. She quickly recovers from the momentary embarrassment.

'I thought we'd stay in. Read, eat together, learn more about each other,' she says, overcompensating to hide her indiscretion.

'Erm, yeah - yeah, of course,' I say, still acutely aware of the slight hint of regret from her earlier foray into premature affection. She unclasps my hand from the piping, allowing it to temporarily hang by my side as she leads me back through to the living room, digging the handle of the knife into the small of my back.

The walk from the bathroom to the front of the flat isn't long at all. The flat itself is quite humbly sized, but she moves slowly, controlling my speed and direction. My body feels exhausted, and each slide of my feet along the carpeted floor requires almost all of my energy. As we walk, I notice that each and every door to every room in the flat has two sets of locks, the same as the bedroom. A strange mixture of padlocks and slightly rusted bolts litter the flat as a reminder of Sarah's intent.

We enter the living room, and she pauses to lock the door with another old, copper key and a code. She indicates for me to sit in the navy blue wingback chair in the centre of the room, just behind the table. I don't fight it, not yet. I let her direct me for now, and I perch in the chair as she makes her way over to secure my feet to the wooden legs that poke out beneath the dark blue cushioning, again threading the rope in a figure eight motion around my ankles. The handcuffs are tight around my wrists, but she's left them to rest in my lap rather than wrenching them behind my back. Her hand lingers for a few uncomfortable seconds on my knee, and she finally turns to sit in the chair opposite me.

She descends heavily, flinging her legs over the arm to face me and grabs a book from the windowsill. There's a small stash of novels piled on the coffee table closest to me. She nods to them, gesturing for me to grab one of my own. I manage to stretch to reach the closest one and begin flicking through the pages.

***

We're sat together in the chairs that I specifically placed in this room. We're just enjoying each other's company, and it's glorious. I knew he'd start to come around, eventually. It will take time, I know that, but he'll love me soon enough. And then we can start to live a normal life, without the restrictive ties and binds.

It's funny to think just how much this room has changed since a mere handful of days ago. Now there are two of us sat here, where there was only ever one before. Two of us here, enjoying each other's company. Two of us happy to be here. I let the time pass quickly as we sit in silence, swept up in the happiness that's filled the room, both getting wilfully lost in the pages of our books.

The narrative has started to lose its hold on my attention. I swing my legs under my torso and arch my back over the arm of the chair, leaning my face nearer to his. He smells sweet and warm, and the closer I get, the more I can smell the undertones of honey on his skin. He turns his head away from his book to meet my gaze and, for the first time since being here, he lets me place my lips on his. It's not overly romantic, but he doesn't flinch and he doesn't pull away. He's still quite stiff, reluctant to allow himself to feel. I lean in and kiss him again, harder this time, absorbing the balmy scent of his skin. I pull away and watch him for a second, still trying to absorb the realisation that he really is here, that he really is with me.

'I'm gonna grab another coffee--want one?'

He nods, turning his attention to the book open in his lap as I leave the room. I look back briefly on my way out and catch him watching me.

Liam

She's left me alone for a few minutes. She left the room, and the tension and awkwardness followed her, dragging behind her like a translucent billowing sheet. So, I've got just a moment to breathe and relax and compose myself before she returns. Just a minute to gather my thoughts and think for myself.

The book I opened this morning remains largely unread. It's sat open on my lap, but I've not digested a single word. I've been staring at the lines of text for what could be hours, or minutes, but none of them have gone in, none of them are memorable. I've just flipped the pages every now and then, to make it look believable.

Now that I'm alone, I start to take in the room more. I've come to realise that the pictures throughout the flat are really odd. Most of them are of different people, but they all look eerily strange. Staged, perhaps. I can't really tell. I've been fixated on one picture virtually all afternoon. Sarah thinks I've been reading I'm sure, hooked on the latest lawyer drama paperback from the Oxfam down the road. In reality, I'm peering over the nicotine stained pages, staring at the biggest picture on the fireplace. It's of a woman and a man standing underneath a silver birch tree, holding hands and kissing. It's romantic, but it's also false. Something about it doesn't ring true. They're both wearing perfectly pressed clothes standing amongst the freshly cut grass, not a hair out of place. It's disconcerting.

The other images are full of people who look remarkably similar to each other, but surprisingly nothing like Sarah. They're all in similar poses, pulling similar faces, wearing similar clothes but with no real expression. And all of the images have been taken in the most beautiful surroundings; open meadows, trickling streams, and towering historic monuments. The photographs mock me from their pedestals and plinths, hanging from the walls and teasing me for my failing memory. I know them. I know these people. I know the faces they're pulling and the emotions they're refusing to convey. The images laugh at my inability to recall their names and their identities. I long to take a closer look but my shackles make sure that remains impossible for the time being.

My stomach growls to remind me how hungry I am. Sarah is considerably smaller than me, and she feeds me as if I'm the same size as her. It's starting to take its toll, draining my attention span, making me gradually weaker and weaker and more and more tired.

'Good book?' Sarah's question breaks my train of thought and draws my attention back to her face. She hands me another mug which I nurse in my hands on top of the book, wishing it was food and not yet more coffee.

'Yeah, it's alright,' I respond. 'Is someone in your family a photographer? The photos in here are great - really professional looking,' I probe.

Sarah shrugs, sitting back down in her armchair. 'No,' she replies. 'Just family snaps from holidays and things. Nothing special.'

Her nonchalant reply confuses me. It baffles me that she doesn't seem to care much for the photos of her family. Why would you cover your walls in images of them to shrug off their presence when questioned?

'They really are good. That one on the fireplace, the one under the tree—where was that taken?'

'What? Oh. I don't know. St. James's Park or somewhere, I think. It doesn't really matter.' She brushes off the question again. It's quite clear that she doesn't want to be pushed on this, but I'm too intrigued to let it rest.

'It's funny how none of your family look anything like you. Actually, none of them really look related to each other.' I speak at her, and this time there's no reply. 'I've always thought I look like the odd one out in my family,' I say, trying to open Sarah up to the conversation and not seem so intimidating. 'They really don't look too similar though. It's odd, isn't it? Are you sure you're not adopted? I bet you heard that joke all the time as a child.'

'I said I don't know, Liam, okay? I don't want to talk about it so leave it. Okay?'

Her anger shattered the atmosphere in the room, sudden and violent. She brought the closest novel up to her face and plunged the room into a tense, icy cold silence. As soon as I'm not cuffed and tied to the next available chair, I'll be taking a closer look at those photographs. They're too strange to not mean anything. And her violent outburst has just confirmed that for me.

'Sarah, I'm sorry, I didn't mean to upset you.'

'Liam! Leave it!' She's up out of the chair, her face now inches from mine. The violence and threat in her eyes is genuine. Her breath is hot and thick against my face. I don't have a chance to respond to her–her hands are around my throat, stifling any response I may have had, dragging my head up away from my neck. Her words are slick and slow. The heat pulsates off her face, her eyes locked in a deep stare with mine.

'I ask the questions–understand?'

My pupils widen in horror as she takes a step back, lowering herself back into her chair as if nothing had happened. I'm stunned. I'm completely bewildered and can't physically bring myself to say anything. I'm terrified of what she might do to me but also of how intrigued I'm becoming by her. I truly don't understand why anyone would react in the way that she just did to pictures of her family that she's chosen to plaster her walls with. What did her family do to her? Worse still, what did she do to her family? What has made her this way–so broken, unstable and volatile? And why should I be so fascinated when she's clearly a threat?

What is she hiding?

Chapter Sixteen

Routine is so easy to slip into. It's been a little over 48 hours, and I already feel like we're making our own orders for things. I lay the table again, only today I feel considerably better about doing it. Despite the outburst earlier and Liam's unnecessary, intrusive questioning, I feel more hopeful, buoyant even. I don't know what brought on his interrogation, but we're past it. It won't be repeated.

He's sat at the table waiting for me to bring the food over. I say sat like he's got much of a choice, but of course, he doesn't. He's still tied to the chair, still cuffed and still shackled, but maybe looser than yesterday. We might be getting better, getting closer to trusting one another, but we're definitely not at that stage yet.

Dinner goes swimmingly. There's no mention of the photographs, no prying questions and interrogation styled quizzing. No signs of him wanting to pry invasively into my private life. I shuffle my chair around to sit closer to him, to be as close as I could be to him. I repeat the actions of the night before, cutting up Liam's food, taking care of him like he needs to be taken care of. I slide a small piece of beef onto the fork.

'There's really no need to look so embarrassed,' I say, holding the food up to Liam's face. 'If you'd just behaved in the first place, you wouldn't be in this situation, would you?'

I'm smug about it; I don't hide the self-satisfied grin and instead let it spread across my face. He blushes, embarrassed, dehumanized perhaps, but he doesn't resist. He opens his mouth, his eyes turned away from mine, staring intently at the floor. He takes the food, awkwardly chewing it as I watch, finally swallowing. It's hard to watch. It's hard to see him acting like a caged animal, trapped in the headlights, staring at me as if I'm some kind of monster. Like I'm his captor, and he's a helpless, defenceless prisoner. I don't want to hurt him, of course I don't. I'd never want to hurt him; I want to love him, and I want him to love me. He'll understand soon enough that, whenever I hurt him, whenever I lash out, it's for his own good. If I ever hurt him, it's his own fault. He'll need to learn to keep his wandering eyes and irritating questions to himself.

I feed him another bite and another until there's nothing left. Just enough food to sustain a man of his build and weight, but less than he's used to, I'm sure.

'There,' I say, dabbing at his face and the corners of his mouth with a napkin. My hand lingers temporarily on his cheek, and I pull it away quickly. I let it fall next to Liam's, brushing past his fingers, sending a trickle of electricity up my arms. His fingers lace around mine, tugging on my hand and pulling me back towards him. He stops for a split second to look deep into my eyes, but they're not full of warmth or affection - I'm not sure they're full of anything at all. Before I quite catch up with what is happening, his lips have met mine. They're exactly how I had imagined they would be during our first kiss: soft and full of energy. It's just a quick kiss, more than a peck, but not bursting with passion. It has taken me completely by surprise, and before I know it, he's kissing me again, harder, stronger this time. His lips peel mine apart, his warm, wet tongue brushing past mine. I close my eyes and give in to the moment. I don't care about his empty eyes, not whilst we're kissing, not whilst everything feels so perfect. He's got me right where he wants me.

Everything is beginning to fall into place. This is what love feels like, I think. Warmth and passion and love and romance and cool, harsh steel. My eyes flash open to meet Liam's stare. My fingers brush past the cold steel of the handcuffs, grazing over the metal that has him trapped, held into place. Their icy touch brings my mind crashing back to the room, back to seeing Liam again for how he really is–strapped to a chair and hopeless. And there they are again, his cold eyes. Not an ounce of emotion threading between his irises. There's nothing there at all.

'I like this a lot more than us fighting,' I say, still holding his hand. I can't help but grin. My expression is mirrored almost exactly back to me; a thin smile, delicate against his chin.

But the smile still doesn't seem to translate to his eyes.

Liam

I kissed her after dinner. A real, convincing kiss. The first was a shy, reserved peck on the lips. The second kiss was more realistic. It took even me by surprise. I pulled her face close to mine, nestling our noses together and kissed her passionately– truthfully. The truth of the kiss, the sincerity of it, shocked me. It momentarily knocked me off my feet. God, how cliché.

My mind is a mess. A heap of jumbled emotions. Terror. Confusion. Paranoia. And now passion? I need to convince Sarah that what I feel is genuine, but I don't want to actually let myself feel anything. I can't let her have that kind of power over me. She can't have the upper hand. Remembering it, remembering how it felt, how it made me feel, makes my stomach churn. The acidic burn of vomit and worry climb up my throat, the long, sticky tendrils of nausea. None of this is normal. None of this is okay.

She fed me again today, like a toddler incapable of looking after myself and completing even the simplest of tasks. She cut up my food and fed me. She even wiped my mouth afterwards with a napkin, like my Nan used to when I was small. I could virtually hear the steam trains edging closer towards my mouth, mocking my age. It's all so surreal. It's like completing benign, daily tasks with thick, woolly gloves on, only obviously I can't move my hands. Everything feels padded and coated in a layer of bubble wrap. I'm alive, but I'm no longer living, no longer permitted to decide anything for myself.

We're back in the bedroom now, sat back on the same hard wooden chair with the same harsh ropes tying my feet to the legs and the same blanket over my lap. She still has the blade. It's back on the bedside cabinet now, so no longer under her pillow, which I consider a small achievement. I look at her as she lies there in front of me. I see her eyes, her hair pulled back from her face, her face clean of makeup and I see an element of vulnerability. I truly think I can get through to her, but right now I'm struggling to think any sense through the exhaustion that seems to be weighing down constantly on my mind.

'Soon you can join me,' she says, her head placed on top of her hand on the pillow. 'Soon we can be sleeping together in this bed. Our bed,' she repeats, her hand patting the soft, silky duvet. She is actually quite beautiful, despite it all. Her face is ethereal in the light of the bedroom, her features slender and delicate and her eyes piercing.

'I know it can't be very comfortable for you on that chair all night, but you must understand. I can't chance anything right now. There's really no alternative. You do understand, don't you?'

'I do understand.' I'm not just saying that to appease her. I genuinely think I understand to an extent. And I feel I'm getting to understand her a whole lot more the longer I'm here, the more I talk to her. Though she's not making it easy to decode her actions, to decipher the meaning behind her words.

We've reached another level today. I watch her as she allows herself to sleep before I've nodded off. She doesn't hesitate tonight. She doesn't force herself to lay awake and stare at me until she's satisfied that I've dropped off. She's exhausted, and she allows herself to close her eyes in front of me. She's letting down her guard.

This woman, who successfully tricked me into her flat, fooled me into believing she was in some kind of trouble, in serious danger, strapped me to a chair. This woman who followed me around and watched me from her seat in the coffee shop for months on end now has me held prisoner. All in the name of love. I watch her as she drops into a deep sleep, her limbs twitching as she falls out of consciousness. I often wonder what she's dreaming about, what it is that's on her mind. Does she dream at all?

Maybe I'll ask tomorrow.

"Who is that?"

The old woman flicks her head up to meet my gaze. Her eyes are tired, her face lined with stress and worry.

'Why, don't you recognise him?' She frowns as she asks me this, like I'm supposed to know who it is on the floor. Like it's obvious or something.

I look harder for a few minutes. I don't think I do know who it is. Though, I suppose there is something oddly familiar about him. His face has a silvery grey undertone, slick and sickly looking. There was once colour in his cheeks, I'm sure, but I watch it now as it spills from his neck, gushing free from a jagged gauge in his throat.

There's something bright and yellow jutting out at a right angle, like a diving board against the grass and the dirt. It's the screwdriver, the silver of the cool metal buried far within the flesh of his neck.

There's blood pooled under his head, cradled behind his ears. His eyes are barely open, but I can make out the blue, cold irises. They're just like mine. His pale skin is dusted with freckles that sink into his cheeks as the life lifts from his chest.

The sight of him should scare me, I think. But I'm more confused than scared. I know I should know more about this situation; I can feel the knowledge of what's happened, the truth of it all, stuck somewhere in my mind, hidden behind a wall of fog.

'I don't remember,' I say, looking again at the old lady. 'Should I know?'

The old lady doesn't answer. She goes back to fussing over the boy, paying him a lot more attention than she ever bothers to pay me. I watch as she brushes his sticky hair from his forehead, her old, calloused fingertips grating roughly over his skin.

'You really ought to know who this is. Do you really not remember? Don't you know what happened?' There's not an ounce of concern in her voice. Her mouth opens and closes but the voice that seeps out is robotic and rehearsed, insincere and false.

She stares at me.

'You did this.'

The fog in my mind thickens and swallows my voice. How could I have done this? Why would I? The fog is asphyxiating and dries up my mouth and tongue as heat floods over my neck and face.

'I--I don't remember,' I say, frantically looking at the boy, searching for clues that will make this make any sense. 'I didn't hurt anyone. I don't understand.'

She doesn't answer me. She just continues to stare.

'I didn't do anything, Grandma. I know this wasn't me,' I shout, wiping my palms across my face, smearing salty tears into my mouth. 'I can't have done this,' I scream. 'I can't!'

The old lady watches me as I cry, hysterical burning tears and snotty sobs. I recognise her, I know that she's my Grandmother, but I feel no emotional connection to her whatsoever. She's right there, but it's as if she's stood behind inches and inches of thick glass. Her eyes are calculating and calm - I can see her thinking, deciding the most logical move to make next.

She turns her back to face the boy again, brushes a stray hair from his eyes and sweeps a single finger over his forehead.

I can see her breathing, sense her contemplating, yet still, she says nothing to me. I'm merely inches away from the terrible scene, but it feels so much farther.

I consider leaving her and running off but just as I decide to move, she turns and speaks to me.

"You did this. I stood here and I--I watched you do this."

I'm shaking my head, whispering 'no' under my breath. The old lady stands up, wiping the boy's blood on the thigh of her skirt. She hobbles over to me, over the boy and through the inches of transparent glass. She places the palm of her hand under my chin and starts to try to comfort me, mumbling under her breath.

'You need to make this right. We can't leave him like this, can we?'

I shake my head again. She's right - he looks so sad, so fractured and twisted on the grass, like a small toy dropped from a great height.

'I know you don't remember doing this, dear. But I saw you do it. With my own eyes. You need to help me clear up this mess; do you understand?'

Her hand is in mine, now. She is tugging gently and pulling me down to the ground, closer and closer to the boy's face.

'Do you understand?' She repeats.

I nod. I don't think I do understand. I don't know what she's expecting me to do to make this better, but I agree regardless.

Her hand is over mine, her coarse, old skin abrasive against my fingers. I flinch as I realise she's pulling me closer to the yellow plastic jutting from his neck. I don't know what she's doing, and I don't feel I can resist as she curls my fingers around the shiny object standing to attention from his throat. She forces my fingers tighter and tighter around the hard plastic. She's looking between me and the boy, the boy then me, whispering under her breath.

'I'm always responsible for clearing up your mess,' she whispers. 'I'm always the one left behind. This is too far, too far.'

'Grandma,' I cry, as her fingers grip mine unbearably tight around the sharp edges of plastic. 'Grandma, please,' I hear myself beg between snotty cries of pain and grief. Suddenly she's let go, but my hand is still gripping the tool and I'm frozen, inches away from the boy's lifeless face, my hand smeared in his blood.

'Pull it out', she commands. 'I said pull it out! Do it now, you silly girl. Do as you're told! Pull it out!'

I'm too stunned to move at first, but she continues to yell. I just want her to stop yelling. I just want to walk away. I try to pull it, but it won't budge. The flesh has relaxed around the metal, hugging it and holding onto it, sealing itself around the foreign object.

'Do as you're told,' she screams again, over and over.

I smack my other hand flat against his cheek, fingers splayed out against his face and just below his ear. I turn my hand over on the handle of the screwdriver to get a better grip and, pushing my weight against his head, I wrench the tool from between the bones in his neck. The release expels an awful popping noise, a slapping sensation as the disturbed flesh tries to seal itself around the wound. The noise—oh the noise it makes. My stomach churns, acid rushing up my throat. I swallow back vomit and blink the tears from my eyes. The darkest blood is spilling from the gaping hole, spilling into a scarlet lake on the floor. I'm crying so hard, so hysterically, that I'm struggling to breathe.

'I know you didn't mean to hurt him, darling,' the old lady says, placing her hands on my shoulders and turning me away from his body. 'I saw it all. He was so annoying, wasn't he? Crying and always getting his way and then there was you, alone and ignored. You just wanted some attention. That's all you ever wanted. You just wanted someone to look at you, to look after you.'

The fog refuses to lift from my mind, memories and recollections refusing to budge to the forefront of my consciousness. I'm so confused, still.

'No, I--I really didn't do anything. I didn't do anything wrong. I don't know what happened!' I choke the words between sobs, watching as *my Grandmother's face hardens. She pulls a handkerchief from her top pocket and wraps it around the handle of the screwdriver, prying it from between my fingers. Droplets of deep red slip off the metal, spattering onto the blades of grass below.*

'We don't have long to get this right, do you understand?'

I didn't understand. I don't understand. I'll never understand. I can't bring myself to speak. I just stare blankly at her weathered face in the hopes that some of this will soon make sense. Any second now.

'Okay, fine. Let's go over it again, Emily. He annoyed you. He wouldn't keep quiet, and the noise was distressing and upsetting to you. You asked him to quieten down, but he wouldn't. You asked him again, and he started teasing you, getting louder and louder, shouting at you and mocking you. So you grabbed the screwdriver that you pocketed from the shed, and you stabbed him with it. In the neck. And then you stood there and you watched him as he bled to death. Do you understand? You didn't want to hurt him, you just wanted him to be quiet.'

She stops and stares at me, waiting for me to understand her words. I know I can't remember exactly what happened, but I don't want to accept what she is saying. I couldn't possibly have done this. I don't know what reaction she is hoping for - what she expects me to do. But it terrifies me that I don't know what happened. I try to search in my memory for what really happened, but all I know is, I didn't do this.

Chapter Seventeen

Hot water pools up behind my neck, flooding around my ears and spilling over my shoulders. It sits in a small lake between my collarbones, nestling on top of my skin. Water has always relaxed me in a way that no other thing can. The liquid flooding around my body, making its way between my toes, nestling behind my kneecaps. I'm inches away from complete relaxation. I concentrate on the water lapping at my hips as I shift my weight, focus on it running off my thighs, rippling over every inch of my body. Every now and then it brims up above my ears, rendering me hard of hearing, like I'm listening to the world through a bubble. It's washing over my torso, warm and therapeutic, the tide dragging me out of consciousness as I drift.

Without warning, the water turns icy cold and is biting at my skin. Someone's hand is around the back of my neck, holding my head under the current like a vice. I hear laughter. It comes in bursts as the owner of the hand finds great delight in torturing me; dragging me from the depths and plunging me back in.

I know that laugh.

I know whom it belongs to.

Water seeps into my ears, brushing against my eardrums and burning my throat. It's clogging up my nostrils, and I kick out against the tide. I open my eyes, but the water is thick, a brown cloud blossoming as I shift my feet in the sand.

There it is again, the laughter.

The hand is forcing me further into the water, its fingertips pushing into my throat, sand and shells brushing against my cheeks.

How long have I been down here? I panic until I can panic no more. The fight leaves my body, seeping out of my pores in tiny billowing clouds. My body relaxes, and my limbs lose their weight, bobbing to the surface. The hand grabs my shoulder heaving me out of the water and flipping me onto my back. The laughter is loud and continuous now, one long string of maniacal cackling. I look up into the eyes of my older brother, screaming at me for being such a wimp, and not putting up a fight.

The only memories I have of him are bullying me. Teasing me until I cried and ran to our mother—when she was still with us. I lie in the shallow water, wet sand clumping together under my body and matting in my hair, cool water lapping around my ankles.

I slowly come-to, my mind returning to the bathtub and the bathroom and Sarah's flat. The chill of the metal cuff sears my wrist. My body is warm except my right arm, which is suspended out of the water and strapped to the handrail on the side of the bathtub. The memory lifts from my consciousness but the emotions that I felt whilst dreaming stay with me. I feel anxious as I lay in this strange in-between, fully awake but not fully aware. I'm between the vivid memory and this clinical, sterile bathroom, in an odd, cold purgatory.

This is the first day that Sarah has trusted me enough to bathe. She's trusted me enough to untether me from the chair. But not enough to completely free me or to remove the handcuffs.

My eyes are closed, but I can hear her, I can feel her watching me from the bedroom to make sure I don't try anything funny. I should be repulsed, disgusted at the thought of her watching me, but I'm not–not really. I've lost track of how many days I've been here now, of how many times I've slept sat upright in the wooden chair by the bed. Time has taken on a fluid state, flitting between day and night quicker than I can keep track of.

I struggle to lift my head out of the tub to meet her gaze.

'Is it your turn yet?' I call out to her.

She's pretending to read a magazine, holding it open in front of her face, her legs crossed at the knee. I know full well she's been watching me. And I can tell by that glint in her eye that she knows I know.

She walks over, just in her dressing gown, shimmying across the floor towards me. The slit in the dressing gown widens as she walks, flashing a glimpse of her smooth thighs. She kneels down beside the bathtub, her face inches away from mine. She can sense the distress I felt moments earlier.

'You know full well I can't do that, as much as I might like to,' she replies, motioning to the cuff on my wrist, that mischievous glint still in her eye. 'Is everything okay?'

I prop myself up on my elbow to face her. 'I'm fine, I just nodded off,' I reply.

She places her hand on my cheek, stroking her thumb over my face. She offers me her hand to help me out of the bath, but I shrug it off. She's taken away my freedom and my sense of independence in every other element of my life, I think I can manage getting out of a bath without admitting that I need her help.

I slide and fumble like a newborn deer trying to get out of the bath, using my free hand to steady my body as I stand up. She's stood back, leaning against the wall watching again. She's holding out a towel for me, waiting for me to stand on my own. Her lips curl up at the edges in a giggle. It's not a malicious gesture; she's not mocking me. I think she's finding this genuinely funny. A loud laugh escapes her mouth as I continue to slide around in the bathtub, one hand still attached to the silver handrail. Perhaps I should have accepted her help the first time round.

'This is much harder than it looks,' I say, stifling my own laugh. I slip, grabbing the rim of the tub in a panic, still giggling as I fall. Her hands are suddenly on my shoulders steadying me, her eyes bashfully focusing on my face to prevent them from wandering down my torso.

'Here,' she says, shoving the towel at me and unlocking the handcuffs. We walk through to the bedroom, her pushing me along by the small of my back.

I could run now. I could chance it. I could leave if I wanted to. I'm in the perfect position to knock her down and run out onto the street screaming for help. I could go back to my life, go back to my home, go back to my job and live normally again. All it would take is one forceful shove, and I could clear the room for the door. She's made a mistake uncuffing me so early on, putting the knife down somewhere out of sight. I could escape; I *should* escape. So why haven't I? Why am I not running? Why have I just allowed her to walk me through to the bedroom without even trying to pull away?

Sarah

He's almost mine. I've almost got him.

He was free for a few minutes today, free to walk in front of me, free to move unguided and without the threatening sight of the blade that has accompanied his every move until now. He was free to strike me and run, but he didn't. He just walked back to the bedroom, slipped on his trousers and shirt and sat on the chair, virtually volunteering to be shackled and cuffed again. It was all very smooth. I didn't sense an ounce of worry from him. He didn't wish to flee. And that fact, that daunting realisation, scared him more than anything else has since he got here.

My stomach jitters at the thought of him actually developing feelings for me, actually wanting to stay of his own accord. The idea of him finally reciprocating the love I feel for him is overwhelming. I pray this continues. I want to feel loved again.

We're both sat in our armchairs reading. This seems to have become our favourite past-time. Reading and enjoying each other's company. There's no need to talk all the time. The quiet is blissful. He's finally beginning to look at home.

The doorbell rings, shattering the silence in the living room. Liam looks at me expectantly, caught off guard by the intrusive noise of the outside world trying to force its way in. I place my book down calmly, pressing the spine into the arm of the chair and stand up.

'Stay put. Don't make a sound,' I say as I walk out of the living room, closing the door behind me and hiding Liam from sight. I keep calm in front of him, like I'm prepared for this to happen, like I would know what to do if it came to it. But in reality I panic. I rush through the hallway to the front door, racking my brain at who could possibly be standing there. I flick the metal disk away from the eyehole and press my face eagerly towards the wood. My eyes take a second to adjust to the outside light and the alien, golden hue of the sun. The world outside curves around the glass of the eyehole, warped by the concave surface. I flick my eyes to the left and right of the door until I settle on the individual that rang my doorbell. I land on a gentleman, tall and clad in uniform. It takes a few seconds for the reality of whom this is to sink in.

It's a policeman. Of course.

My blood pressure rockets and my palms are immediately sweaty with nerves and anxiety. My heart beats frantically in my ears, my stomach swelling with nausea. I rack my brain for a reason why there could be a policeman stood on my doorstep and how–*if*–they could possibly know about Liam. I swallow back the sting of vomit and let the copper disk fall back over the small glass bubble that separates me from him.

Just breathe. One, two three.

I drag my sweaty palms down my jeans, desperately trying to dry them off and wipe the nerves away. I unlock the door, opening it just enough to see the officer and allowing him to see me. A cool stream of air seeps in through the open door, the freshness of it stinging my nostrils. I compose myself, holding my head up to the stranger in an attempt to look confident yet understandably concerned at his being here.

'Can I help you?'

The voice that leaves my mouth doesn't sound at all how I feel. It's confident and level, in stark contrast to the frenzy and hysteria that's buzzing in my brain, bouncing between my ears. The vague notes of concern are there in my tone, but the officer just stares, his hands by his sides and his radio crackling with life on his belt.

'Yes, maybe you can. Sorry to bother you so late in the evening. There's been a missing person's report filed in your area. We're just knocking a few doors, seeing if anyone's seen or heard anything.'

I stare at him, unsure if his last sentence indicated that I needed to respond or if it was a purely rhetorical question. I wait for him to carry on.

'We're looking for a Noah Baker. Do you know him?'

I shake my head, lips pursed, eyes focussed on the officer's face. I don't recognise the name. I don't know him from around, but then I don't really know anyone in the area. I've kept it that way deliberately.

'No, I'm afraid I don't. I don't know anyone by that name.'

Another brief pause for effect. This guy knows how to drag out the suspense. He fumbles around in his pocket for a few moments and produces a small photograph of Liam. It looks quite old, maybe a picture from a couple of years ago. It could be even older, perhaps a photo taken at university. There are deep ridges in the printed image where it's been folded numerous times, the colour cracking through the paper. I'd forgotten Liam's actual name. The sight of his face being referred to as Noah catches me off guard.

They know he's missing.

They don't know where he is, and it doesn't appear that they suspect anything of me. I firm my face to hide my realisation that Liam was now known as a missing person and replace it with my best impression of an overly concerned member of neighbourhood watch.

'No, I'm really sorry, I don't recognise him,' I say, shaking my head, pretending to study the image closer.

I look up expectantly, poised and ready for his questions if he does have any more. The police officer fumbles with the photograph, folding it back up and slipping it into his pocket.

He accepts what I have to say without further interrogation - why would he question me? He pulls out a small piece of card from the chest pocket of his shirt and hands it to me.

'If you do hear anything or see anything unusual at all, please let me know.' I take the card, not looking at it but running my fingers around the firm edge.

'Of course. Erm—sorry, officer?' He turns back to look at me, halfway back up the drive. 'Is he in danger - the man that's missing? It's just I–I dread to think how his family must feel if he's been missing for so long. And, well, if it's not safe around here--.' I let my question trail off. I didn't mean to ask it, but it slipped out of my mouth before I had a chance to stop it.

'I can't discuss that I'm afraid,' he says, gently shaking his head. 'Though at this stage, it just looks like the young man may have had enough and left town. I wouldn't be too worried. But if you do hear anything, give me a call.'

'Of course, officer. Goodnight.'

I watch him as he trundles up to the pathway, turning left to walk to the next houses along. He doesn't seem concerned. In fact he seems happy to lap up my lies with no need for me to even try to convince him. I take a few breaths with the door open, thankful for the fresh air. I fill my lungs and slide the door closed, leaning my forehead on the wood; still listening to the fading footsteps to make sure that the policeman has well and truly gone. I slip the bolt back across the door, therapeutically sealing all of the locks and closing off the outside world. I give myself a minute to catch my breath and compose myself before going back into the living room.

The police suspect Liam, or *Noah,* is a missing person. They know he's gone. I can't even calculate how long he's been down here now, but I know it must be well over a week, maybe touching two. Not only is he gone, but they also don't know where he is, or what he's doing. They don't suspect me at all.

I'm winning at this.

Power and energy floods up through my stomach and chest. *I'm winning.* Should I be worried or concerned or nervous, or whatever it is I'm meant to be feeling in this situation? Because truly, I'm just not. I'm powerful and confident and influential. I've outsmarted everyone, and Liam is just inches away from realising his feelings for me. He was just inches away from that policeman, but I'm the one who still has him. I'm a perfect model citizen in this town. I'll be sure to ring the number on the card if I do see anything, which I won't, obviously.

I glance down at the card and inspect it quickly. A cheap, beige rectangle of thick paper. It has the local police station's number crudely stamped on it in black ink and presumably the name of the officer I just spoke to pressed underneath. I run my fingers around the edge again, proud of my composure and thrilled that people are looking for Liam. I've got him. He was right in my living room all along, and the Police Officer didn't have a clue. He was none the wiser. Adrenaline shunts through my veins as I walk back into the living room. There he is, sitting in exactly the same position as when I'd left him, still reading, still quiet.

'Who was that?'

'No one - just a neighbour. Wanted to borrow something,' I reply. Lying is second nature, but it does feel harder with Liam. The lie came out awkwardly and fractured, jarring in my mouth. I want to tell him the truth about everything. I want him to know me for who I am, to know me inside and out. But I can't risk that yet, so the white lies will have to continue.

Liam nods, returning to his book. He doesn't believe me, I can tell. I can hear it in the words he doesn't say, but he doesn't press me any further. He lets it go.

I perch on the end of my armchair pretending to read my cheap paperback again, flicking the pages into a fan shape and breathing in the second-hand book smell. I lift my foot up over my knee and place it on his chair, just brushing his leg with it. My limbs tingle with the electricity of the power I have over this man sat beside me. I own him. The world can't have him, because I've decided he's mine.

We sit for a few more minutes, stepping through the evening's routine with ease. Conversation has started to come a lot more easily now - mostly just small talk, but not the forced, interrogating kind. I feel like we're learning to trust each other.

I make dinner. I lay the table as I have done the few nights previous and we sit and eat together. I eat some of my meal first and, once I'm satisfied, I'd pick up the fork and start to feed Liam. He still hates this process, but he hates being weak and tired more, so he takes the food between his teeth without arguing. We make it about two-thirds of the way through the meal with pleasant chatter about nothing in particular, until Liam starts to ask questions.

'That wasn't a neighbour, was it Sarah?' He asks the question in a flat tone, his usual kindness stripped bare.

'What?' I reply nonchalantly, looking up briefly from my plate.

'The person at the door—it wasn't a neighbour, was it?' He lets the question hang limply in the air. I'm not prepared to tell him the truth, even though it's clear that he can sense I'm lying to him. He can smell it on me; he can hear it in my voice. He's not stupid.

'No, it wasn't,' I say, glancing up to meet his eyes over the forkful of food that hovers by his face. 'It was -- it was my Mum. She wanted to speak to me, but I told her I was busy. I'm sorry for lying to you, Liam, but I couldn't have her in here. I can't face her.'

He winced at the second lie, at the use of his name. Even after all this, he's still not quite used to the sound of it out loud, but he's past the stage of arguing it. The second lie hasn't appeased him either. I can see him questioning the logic of it in his face. He's questioning why I would have lied about something like that in the first place, why I wouldn't have had more of a reaction considering how open I'd accidentally been with him regarding my relationship with my mother just a few days ago. I'd stumbled and faltered, and he knew it.

I'm not about to offer him a true explanation, so I focus on taking his mind off the situation entirely. I force our eyes to meet over the plate of food and question if what I'm about to do is a good idea. I place the fork on the side of the plate, still half full of food, and I lay my hands on his cuffed hands lying in his lap. I slip the key out of my pocket, and slowly, intentionally, I unlock them. His right hand slips free onto his lap and remains there. His eyes are frozen and locked into mine, judging the situation and analysing his next move. But he doesn't budge. He doesn't pick up the nearest item of cutlery and throw it at me or attack me or lash out at me. He doesn't push up from the chair and run. He doesn't attack me in any way. He leaves his hand resting in his lap, questioning my motives.

I lean over the table and slide my hand over his, lacing my fingers under his palm and pull his hand up onto the wooden surface next to his plate. I leave his hand next to his fork and sit back. His face is struggling to process what I've done–the slight amount of power I have afforded him. His fingers reach out gradually to take hold of the fork, and he lifts it, as if he has never used such a utensil before. I watch as he rolls the stem of the bronzed fork between his fingers, clearly analysing and questioning what would be the best move for him to make. I can see him fretting and struggling to process the small act of kindness. He stabs the nearest potato, sliding the prongs into the soft flesh. Within a few minutes, he is using it as normal. It's like watching an animal using human cutlery for the first time, the poor creature questioning its power and potential, its purpose. His face is wrought with confusion as he struggles to process my possible motives for helping him like this, but it doesn't take him long to finish what was left on his plate. I watch him as he swallows the last mouthful. As he flicks his eyes up to mine every few seconds, checking on me and checking what I'm doing. I watch him question it all, and I have no intention of explaining my actions to him.

I take the fork and plate from in front of him as he finishes, leaving him with his hand free to roam the table. I walk to the kitchen and grab two cups, pouring in some leftover filter coffee from earlier on in the day. I give myself a minute to breathe out, unwatched. I look around the kitchen, at how clean it is, at how organised and adult it makes me feel. It's almost unbelievable that just a handful of days ago this place looked like a hovel--entirely unrecognisable. I recall the gathered mountains of empty microwave meal boxes, the precariously leaning mugs stacked up like a forgotten game of Jenga. The mould and spores and grime covering every inch of the place. I almost miss the comfort I found in the dirt.

I balance the two mugs on saucers and carry them into the living room on one hand, grabbing a couple of teaspoons and a jar of sugar cubes in the other. I lay them in front of him, in between our two place settings and nod for him to take one. His actions are familiar, though I've not seen them in a long while. He slides the mug towards him, picking out two lumps of brown sugar from the jar and dropping them into his mug. He grabs the teaspoon, which is far too small in his hands, and stirs three or four times. Once finished, the teaspoon is nestled on the side of the saucer, just as I'd expected, with the tiniest amount of brown liquid left in the dip of the metal. He lifts the mug to his face and catches my eye.

'What?' he asks.

I shake my head. 'It's nothing. It's just,. you do that exact same thing every time you have a coffee. It's like the routine is ingrained in you.'

'Do I? I can't say I've noticed.'

I nod, taking a sip of my own coffee.

'You were watching me that closely? In the coffee shop, I mean?'

He doesn't seem shocked or disturbed. He's merely just asking a question. I nod again.

'I couldn't take my eyes off of you.'

Liam

She's freed up one of my hands. It feels alien, being able to move it. It feels unnatural now, like it's been trained to be more efficient whilst strapped to the other one or the arm of a chair. I think she wants me to know that she's beginning to trust me, but I'm still not trusting her. I can't chance it.

I've caught myself a few times in the last couple of days reacting to her as if she's doing me a favour, as if reciprocating her feelings and actually caring are the normal reactions for me to have in this situation. I've caught myself doing it, I've scalded myself, and now I need to lay a plan to get out of here.

I think as she potters around me. I flex my fingers, rolling them around on the surface of the table, playing an invisible piano, stretching the life and movement back into them. I need to bide my time; I can't just bolt the second she starts to free me up.

She's back clearing away the plates in exactly the same manner as last night and the night before that and the night before that. The routine, the dullness, the beige hue this has all taken on infuriates me. I need to speed this up, but I know I need to keep it believable. I need to trick her how she tricked me. Just a few more days are all it should take.

'Sarah?'

I call, and she walks back in, a wet plate in one hand and the damp, twisted tea towel hanging down at her side in the other. She waits for me to speak again.

'I don't care who it was. At the door, I mean.' I let my sentence sink in, watching each individual word processing behind her eyes. It takes a while, but she grins, placing the plate and towel on the table and meandering over to me. She leans down, her hands placed on my knees, and pecks me on the lips. I don't stop myself from kissing her back, and I don't push her away. But I don't let myself feel a thing. I can't afford to.

She leans in again and presses her lips against mine. Her hand makes its way behind my head, her fingers running through my hair, lacing between every strand. I can't feel anything for this woman, but I can't let her question me. My guard needs to stay up, but this needs to be convincing. Her kiss is so sincere and warm; her smell is inviting and homely.

I can't do this.

This is the only time I can guarantee that she isn't lying to me. I know that this is the truth to her. I scrape my mind away; separate it from my lips and the cocktail of confused emotions that are swimming around between our mouths. She's still kissing me, throwing herself at me and I'm answering when I know that I shouldn't be. I can't afford to feel this way.

Her legs swing over my hips as she sits square on my lap and continues to lean in, kissing my lips, caressing my face. Both her hands are cradled behind my head now, her fingers sliding up behind my ears and down around my neck. She means it. She means every kiss, and I'm trying my hardest not to mean a single one. The pit of my stomach tells me that this is the worst thing I could be doing. This is wrong on every possible level. I'm leading this woman down a path that I have no intention or ability to continue down, and yet here I am reciprocating her kisses as if we're long-time lovers. Her body is rocking against mine, her breath hot against my neck as she whispers little butterfly kisses all over my face and behind my ears. I can feel myself giving in, I can feel my guard slipping and my heart throbbing despite the knowledge that this is horrifically wrong weighing down on my shoulders like a casket. She grabs my free hand and places it on her thigh, encouraging me to slip under her spell, dragging my conscience further and further away from my mind. She knows exactly what she is doing and despite my desperate attempts, I can't seem to stop her. The kisses get harder and faster, stronger and more passionate and more truthful by the minute. My body relaxes the more I give into her, the more I let her take over, wrapping around my body like a siren at sea.

She mumbles my name in my ear, her damp breath tickling my throat. Only it's still not my name she's saying—it's Liam. Liam. Over and over again. Who is this Liam? But I don't question—I let her carry on until she says it louder, more meaningfully.

'Liam?' She asks, pulling herself away from my chest and tilting her head at me. 'Liam—I think it's time, don't you?' Her eyes light up waiting for me to answer, expectant.

I don't know what I'm supposed to reply—I don't know what she means. Time for what? Before I can answer, she's unfurling herself off my lap and kneeling at my feet. My heart stops as her hands begin to untie the harsh, coarse rope that has been binding my ankles to this chair for days on end. The ropes slither free onto the floor, tugging at my bare skin for the last time and brushing against the carpet. I flex my ankles, encouraging life back into the stiff joints.

Sarah pushes herself up off the floor and perches back on my knees inspecting my every move, analysing every expression with the intensity of a bird of prey. I don't know what she is expecting me to say, so I play it safe and stay silent, not letting her break eye contact with me.

She's wearing a smug grin, not unattractive but certainly more powerful than I'd like to admit. Her hand traces the remaining handcuff, her fingertips making the lightest movements over the cold metal. Her movements are so light, so delicate and yet so electric. I can feel each individual ridge in the pads of her fingers, each peak and trough in the tip of her nail bed, like it's a grain of wood. My body is frozen to the spot. I daren't move, I daren't speak a word for fear of her panicking and shackling me back to the chair.

I can almost taste the outside world on the tip of my tongue. Not much longer left to play this game, much less time than I thought. She leans her head down into the cradle behind my ear and kisses, tiny gentle kisses, over the crest of my shoulder. Each kiss renders me motionless, freezing me further to the spot. Her lips travel slowly down my arm, trickling down my biceps and burrowing in the soft hammock of my elbow. Each kiss is beautiful and tender and passionate, but each as poisonous as the last. She kisses my wrist, and I can feel her fumbling with the final handcuff below her lips. A shudder ripples across my spine with the building excitement.

I can't see what she is doing beyond the back of her head, but I can feel it. I can feel it so vividly I can almost see it happening through her skull. Her slipping the key from her jeans pocket, sliding it into the minute lock in the cuff at the base of my wrist. The noise is magnified as my senses heighten. The smooth, slick entering of the key, the crunching of the lock as she turns it in the mechanism, the biting of the teeth as they grasp and the shunting of the metal as it finally releases my wrist.

For the first time in I don't know how long, I'm free.

My body tingles, each nerve ending in a pinprick, vibrating on the surface of my skin. The cuffs drop with a clatter to the floor, the light from the lamp bouncing off the shiny metal surface and refracting glowing freckles across Sarah's face. Neither of us reach for them; neither of us react. We just carry on kissing and nestling deeper into each other, one pulsating organism moving in sync. I get completely lost in it, my mind being dragged deeper and deeper into her smell, her movements, her kisses, her voice. It only stops when she decides it can. She pauses, pushing herself away from my chest and holding my face in her hands.

'Liam. I think we're ready now. I'm going to go and get ready, and when I come back, you can come to bed. Okay?'

There's not a hint of nervousness in her voice. Her words are calm and collected and instructive. She's in control, for now. I watch her as she stands up and leaves me perched on the chair, but no longer shackled like an animal. She leaves the room, closing and locking the door behind her, leaving me alone.

***

He's mine, I can feel it. He's given in. I could sense it when we were kissing. It was like kneading bread. At first, he was unresponsive and cold, but the more I worked on him, the more I persevered and showed him that I would love him no matter what he thought, the more he opened up and began to feel the same way for me.

I'm oddly calm now, but the excitement is there, bubbling just millimetres below my skin. In a few moments, I can allow it to fully take over, but I need to remain calm and focused for now. This moment has to be absolutely perfect, everything exactly as I have been imagining it since the day I laid eyes on him in that coffee shop. All those months ago that feel a lifetime behind me now.

I slink out of the room, locking the door from the outside. I know he's mine now, but I can't help the action, the precaution; it's become second nature. The locks slide into place with a cool shunt and I listen to him breathing just for a moment. Those breaths are so far away right now, but soon they'll be gasps and pants just inches from my skin, in time with my own body. I lay my hand on the door for a moment to gather my thoughts, to catch my breath. He's far behind the door but I can feel the electricity from his body through the wooden form, the emotions and the love and the excitement pulsing in my palm.

Everything I have done, everything we have done together has been in preparation of this moment. I walk into the bedroom alone, swinging open the wardrobe door to reveal the black suit bag. I lay it on the bed. The zip slides freely down the length of the dark plastic, revealing the bright splash of colour that I remember. It's exactly how I pictured it:

seductive, sexy, the glow of freshly spilled blood. I throw off my clothes as the trepidation and adrenaline threatens to overcome me, rolling off my socks and throwing my t-shirt over my head onto the floor at the side of the bed. I unlatch the small silk hooks from the wooden hanger, letting the dress remove itself from the bag as if it is a living, breathing thing with a mind of its own. The rich silk glides effortlessly from the hanger. I drag the zip down the length of the back of the dress, listening to every individual tooth run past the next, and slip the dress over my head. The material is cool and soft and clings to my body in all the right places. The red is stunning, made all the brighter against my pale skin. I brush the shiny fabric over my collarbones and allow myself a few minutes to inspect my work in the mirror.

I love him. And he loves me back.

The reality of it glows from my skin. I dab on a bit of red lipstick and pace back to the living room to collect him.

Liam

She's outside the door. I can hear her pulling the locks closed and standing there, listening. I lost it for a moment, when she was kissing me and laying her body all over me. I lost control and so nearly gave into her temptations. But hearing her out there now, hearing her listen to me as the caged animal that I still am, I know that that can't happen. She's volatile and unstable, and I'm very much being held fugitive. And I am closer than ever to getting out of here. I'm disgusted at myself for letting my guard down in that way, for allowing my depraved body to develop feelings of any kind towards this woman.

I can hear her now, in the bedroom. I'm not sure what she's doing, and I try not to let my imagination fill in the blanks. But I can hear her. Hear her breathing and shuffling about and moving around in the room. She's left nothing in here that I can use as a weapon, nothing that I could possibly use to defend myself against her. She's prepared for this. All of the cutlery and plates have gone from the table. Not even a mug or stray fork or a single heavy item in sight. I scour the room in search of anything that I can use to defend myself, to get myself out of here, but there's nothing.

I'm off the chair now, standing in the middle of the room, my knees slightly bent to stop myself from toppling over. My limbs are shaking with a mixture of fear and anticipation and the alien weight of my body pushing down on my thighs. My ears pulsate as I force myself to listen harder, to hear what she's up to. I catch her opening the bedroom door. I sense her walking back to the living room, running her fingers along the wall and humming. I feel her breathing. I hear her sliding open the locks of the living room door, it creasing open a few inches to reveal a bright flash of red, shimmering fabric.

Sarah

I am so ready to see him, so ready for him to see me like this. I virtually run back to the living room to collect him, singing under my breath a jolly tune reminiscent of my childhood. I wonder if my mother would ever be proud of me, if my grandmother would care. If they'd be jealous to see Liam again, to see him happy to be with me and happy to love me. Not scared of me, but in love with me. Not lying on the floor with a screwdriver jutting out of his neck. Probably not. That almost makes it better, that I'm rebelling against them even when they're not here. When they've not been here for me in years.

I lay my hand flat on the door again; ready to see him, excited and anxious for him to see me. I can feel his pulse, his heartbeat, every artery and pulsating vein through the wood of the door. He can feel me too, I know it. I slide open the locks on the door, careful to tease him with just enough of the dress as I do.

Liam

I panic and grab a lamp from the table by her armchair, heaving it from its socket in the wall. Its weight throbs in my hand, the cool ribbed surface pulsating under my fingers. As she enters the room, I lunge at her, shoving my hand into her throat and forcing her back against the door. She's shocked, her eyes wrought with terror. I know the second I make eye contact with her that I shouldn't have looked; I should have just swung for her whilst I had the chance. It only takes her a second to regain her footing and realise what is happening. She pushes against me with all her weight. The lamp slams down onto the crown of her head. She loses her footing and tumbles to the floor, a folded heap of bright red silk at my feet.

I've stopped breathing. I've held all of my breath, trapped it in my lungs in case my breath wakes her up and causes her to stir. I need to move her from the doorway; I need to get out of here. My legs are shaky and stiff, my joints protesting at being straightened and used for the first time in over a week, maybe longer. I force myself forward onto my knees, placing my hands under her torso and, with all the energy I can muster, drag her away from the door. The silk of the dress allows me to move her with ease and she slides over the carpet into the centre of the room. She looks peaceful lying there. It's refreshing to see her so defenceless, but I know how dangerous she can be. I know now what she is capable of.

I tear my eyes away and hurl my body through the door. Harsh white light fills the hallway, reflecting off the neutral walls and carpet. I swear I only hesitate for a second. One split second to take a breath as I gather myself and shove my feet into some shoes on the wire rack by the door. I don't even risk a glance over my shoulder, not even to check she's still there. It was just a second. But that second was enough for her to regain consciousness. That one second I take to orient myself and coordinate my escape has given her enough to rise up on her hands and knees.

The fall has sent her hair tumbling over her face and shoulders in knotted, twisted clumps of dark brown rope, barely hiding her rabid expression. Her eyes lock into mine, brows furrowing into a deep frown, bright scarlet lipstick smudged around her lips.

I stumble forwards. My hands are on the front door now. I can feel the fresh air; I can smell it. My mouth waters with its taste. The first lock untwists with ease and my hands immediately vacate to the second, the cool metal beneath my fingers pulsating with energy and hope.

'Liam,' she yells at me as I leave, screaming and bellowing, the noise emanating from the pit of her stomach. 'Liam!'

I turn my head to take one last glance before running into the street. She's on her feet, bounding towards me with inhuman energy.

'I won't let you leave me, Liam. Not again!' I flick the bolt across, twisting the key simultaneously and heave the reinforced door towards me. I can see it, I can literally smell the outside world. My face is out; one hand is out.

'No!'

Her animalistic cries ring in my ears, bouncing off the inside of my head, volleying between my ears. My body slams into the solid wood of the door. She's on my back. Her hands close around my throat as she screeches inaudibly, split flying from between her teeth.

'I will not let you leave!'

She grabs a fist full of hair at the root, her nails scraping against my scalp and peeling up the skin in her fingernails. My neck flings back with her pull, my head yanked back into the blackness of the flat. Her fingers have a vice-like grip on my skull, controlling my body and sending my limbs into a frenzy. Still screeching, she forces her arm straight behind my head, sending my face flying through the air back towards the door. It makes contact with the wood with the most horrifying crack. I'm vaguely aware that the crunch of bone I've just heard emanated from my own face, my own nose crumpling and retreating into the shelter of my cheeks. Hot, sticky blood gushes from my nostrils, flowing off my chin and seeping into the woven fabric of my shirt. It's damp and warm; it's clinging to my chest, the red printing onto my skin. I glance down. The blood is billowing out, a bright red flower displayed on my chest like a badge of honour. I don't feel the pain at first, just the shock at the power behind her arms, the anger in her chest. I don't feel pain, just a strange, out of body hollowness. I flick my eyes up to meet hers, to see her dilated pupils and crazed expression. The pain seeps into my bones, an intense burning that makes my eyes water uncontrollably. Her hands are up at my shoulders again in an instant, shoving my body towards the door. She's screaming, shrieking, but the pain is muting everything, muffling her shouts and yells. She shoves me with all her might, but I weigh my body to the ground and try my best to shake her off. The blow to my face has knocked any ounce of strength I had left. I taste blood, the rich iron filling my mouth. I can smell it at the back of my throat. In a desperate attempt, I reach for the door again.

Chapter Eighteen

'I love you. I can't let you go!'

The screams shudder through the hallway scorching her throat and tearing at her larynx. It's a miracle no one from the outside world heard all the commotion, the chaos in the tiny one bedroom basement flat. The fibres in her voice box fray against the tirade of screams. It's a wonder no one noticed that she's not left the flat in over a week, that she's not been to work, that she's not opened a window or even the front door to check for mail.

The dark-haired woman has hold of the bloodied man by the scruff of his neck, piling his body, face first, into the front door. Her movements are precise and calculated, pre-decided perhaps. Maybe conjured from the pages of those crime novels that are piled up high in her bedside cabinet. She grabs hold of him again shoving her weight against his torso and piling his face into the door, over and over again, her biceps flexing and glistening with sweat, his face dripping with crimson splatters of blood. His face makes a loud, discerning crunch as it contacts the polished wooden door, his features slowly losing their rigidity and collapsing into their sockets. His eyes are swollen beyond recognition, puffy and full of liquid and purpling with bruises. She grabs at him again, but he manages, somehow, to break free and launch his body at her, the momentum sending her crashing to the floor. She falls, the life taken out of her body like a deflated windsock, her head and neck ricocheting off the banister that lead up the mini flight of stairs into the hallway. She's just laying there now, her neck twisted at a strange angle, her face pale and peaceful against the bloodied carpet. He's fallen to his knees beside her, the momentum and energy flooding from his pores onto the floor. He struggles for a minute, tries to stand back up. Now is his perfect opportunity to leave, to struggle with the door for a few seconds and lunge out onto the street crying for help, screaming for his freedom and his home and his mundane job and his disinterested companions. He lays his hand on the door and tries to stand. The energy has gone. It has seeped out of every orifice in his body and now lies in a pool of exhaustion at his feet. Against his better judgement, against his mind and every fibre of his being, he is giving up. Though freedom waits for him on the other side of a single door, he's lost the will to keep fighting. The life has all but completely escaped from his body, and he passes out in a tangled heap on the floor next to the woman in the red dress.

***

We stand there staring at the little boy's body for what feels like hours on end. I can't peel my eyes away from the hole in his neck and the darkening, congealing halo sticking to the grass around his head.

I do know him. I know that now.

'Grandma, what did you do? What really happened?' I wait for a response.

'I told you. You had an accident, remember? It's okay. You won't get into trouble, you'll just need to...go away, for a while. Do you understand?'

I shake my head. I don't. The fog is closing and getting denser. I glance at my mother who has been silent throughout this entire exchange. She's kneeling on the floor next to the body, not saying a word, not looking up or moving. She's motionless. I panic momentarily, concerned that I've stabbed her too. That I've attacked and murdered my own mother, and I somehow have no recollection of it.

'Mum?' I call for her, but she doesn't answer. She turns her head silently to look at me, her eyes brimming with fresh tears, her face stained red and sore by old ones. It's clear in her face that she's distraught, that whatever this is has torn her apart. But there's something else below the surface that I can't put my finger on.

Her hands are covered in blood. Not the bright red kind, more the kind that's started to brown and dry up in the air, crisping at the edges. It's all over her fingertips, clotting under her fingernails, entrenched in the ridges of her palms like dirt. She's wiped her hands on her jeans, smeared the gore into the light blue denim and dragged it up the length of her thighs. 'Mum?' I call again, but she continues to stay mute, absentmindedly peeling the drying blood from her knuckles and her nail beds.

'Your mother has nothing to do with this, dear. She just needs you to tell the truth. She's very upset.'

My mother is crying again, louder now for me to hear. Her eyes want to tell me the truth; she wants to be free of whatever is burdening her. The guilt is smeared over her face as clear as the blood across her jeans. She's desperate.

I walk closer to her. I want to hug her, to tell her it's going to be okay, though I'm not sure what it is that I'm assuring her of. I take a step closer, and she yells.

'No! Emily, stay where you are!'

I can't help the confusion; it spreads across my face like wildfire. What have I done? What has she done?

I walk further towards her, ignoring her cries. Grandma seems to have faded into the background; her skin has taken on a watery, semi-translucent quality. She's just standing to the side and waiting for us to argue or cry or whatever it is we're about to do.

'Emily, I--I need to tell you something.'

Grandma cuts her up, placing her hand on her shoulder to quieten her. 'Joyce,' she growls. 'Just let the girl understand what she has done so we can get on with this. This is the best way,' she hisses through gritted teeth. 'You need to trust me.'

'I can't lie, Mum. I can't. I just can't.' Her head is in her hands, her words muffled by cascading tears and sobs.

'Mum, what is it?'

'Emily. You didn't hurt him. I did. . I couldn't stop him crying. He just wouldn't stop crying. I couldn't make him understand me, and I lost it. I'm sorry, I lost control.'

I've never seen my mother like this before. She's shuddering from the weight of the tears, the tears that are ripping through her body, tearing her apart from the inside out. Her words are hard to understand, dotted between bellowing sobs and cries and shrieks. She's hysterical.

'I killed him, Emily. I killed your brother, and I'm so, so sorry.'

The strength in my legs disappears. My knees give way to the weight of my body, and I catch myself just as I crash to the floor next to the boy. I do recognise him, of course I do. Why did I not see this before, behind the blood and the sweat and the mud smeared across his face? Behind it all, of course. It's my brother. My younger brother who's only just learnt to write his own name, only just mastered throwing a ball and chasing after me in the garden, who can only just use a knife and fork. I look down at him again, past the blood and the grime and into his staring, vacant eyes. A nauseating sting courses up my throat and rests at the back of my tongue.

'Liam?' No one responds. My Grandma continues to stare, her arms now folded across her chest and looking down at my mother, waiting for her to answer me. 'Mum, I'm scared. What do we tell Dad? What happens now?'

She tries to answer, but the sobs have fully taken over, leaving her completely speechless. Her back judders from the weight of what she has done. My Grandma places her hand on my mother's back and turns to face me. Her expression is stern, business-like.

'Emily, listen,' she says as I try to reach my mother, to comfort her. 'Emily, you need to listen to me. Can you do that?'

I nod. I don't know what else to do. I might not like her, but my Grandma is the only one that is speaking in full sentences. I'm glad to have someone here that seems to know what to do.

'Emily, you need to act like you've done this. You can't let your mother take the blame for this; she wasn't in her right mind.'

I want desperately to tell her that I can't do that; how can she expect me to? I want nothing more than to yell at her and say no, but the words have wedged themselves deep in my throat, and I can't muster much more *than a dry croak. I try again to speak over her, to cry out, but she holds her hand to my face.*

'Emily, don't make me yell at you. Don't make this any worse than it already is. Your mother cannot take the blame for this.' Her voice is stern and strong, as if she'd prepared for this day. 'She's not well. If you own up, if you say you did this, then you'll just need help. You'll go away for a while to be taught how to act, how to think and how to behave. And we all know that this wouldn't be the first time you've had a violent outburst. It's not the first time you've done something horrific, Emily. But if your mother owns up to this, then she'll go to prison for the rest of her life. She'll die there. She'll die in prison, with the murderers and rapists and horrible, horrible guilty people. And she's not guilty, is she? Is she, Emily? Do you want your mother to die in prison? Do you want to be responsible for that?'

I can't answer. I'm shocked and terrified and sick and horrified at what this woman is saying to me.

She steps over the body as if it wasn't there, lunges past my mother and grabs me by the shoulders. Her bony, old fingers dig deep beneath my shoulders, into the gap in my collarbone, making me cry out in pain. I try to shake her off, but she's a big lady, and her fingers have locked into my joints like a vice. She kneels down, her face inches from mine.

'Your mother cannot go down for this. If she goes to jail and dies in there, that will be your fault - her death will be on you too. Do you understand, Emily?'

My face screws up with floods of burning hot tears. I can't possibly be about to agree to this. This wasn't my fault. I did nothing. My mother literally just admitted to murdering my brother, but I can't let her be guilty of this. I can see in her eyes that she did it, but she's not guilty. She's as confused as I am.

The old woman grabs my shoulders and shakes me, throwing my head back and forth. 'You need to get this, Emily. This will be a damn sight easier if you just admit it and take responsibility. Understand?' I don't answer her. I stare instead at the phlegm hanging from her yellowing teeth and focus on keeping myself upright as her fingers continue to press themselves into my shoulders.

'We all know that this isn't the first time you've done something like this. Everyone knows of your violent tendencies, Emily. You hardly hide the outbursts, your anger, your rage. Don't forget that.'

Those words will stay with me for a long time. I know they'll shape the way I act for the rest of my life if I let them.

I walk the few remaining steps to my mum, kneel down and pull her arm over my neck. I lay there for a few minutes, listening to her heartbeat, breathing in her familiar, warm scent whilst I still can. I grip her torso with my arms, hugging her and soaking in the last of her love that I can muster.

'I killed Liam, Mum. I'm so, so sorry.'

Chapter Nineteen

The two of them lay there peacefully, in an oddly grotesque and detached way. The woman is sprawled on the ground, her toes pointed towards the door, and her legs bent in an unnatural plié. She looks small, twisted in her ballet pose on the floor. He lays next to her, crumpled and muscular, his face full of pain and anguish. They rest there together, a pair of tiny dancers dropped from a great height, a pair of forgotten toys kicked to the side of the room to be picked up later.

The hallway is silent and eerie. No sound whatsoever, not from the inside or the outside. Just the gentle, strained breathing from the pair on the floor, struggling to get enough breath to sustain themselves. The beautiful red dress has been torn in the commotion. It has split up one leg revealing a thigh and new, flourishing bruises from the tumble. She always did argue with those she was close to. She has a bit of a history for it, a long chequered past of screaming, brawling rows and fists flying through the air. He doesn't at all. He's got a peaceful, suburban upbringing but gets bored quickly. He left his family behind some time ago.

His eyes start to roll around in their sockets. They move with the growing pain in his face, flitting from side to side, sandpaper against the thin film of the lids.

The bedroom door is open as she'd left it just a few minutes before. The bed is freshly made, the curtains drawn, her dirty clothes dragged into the wash basket. She'd made sure everything was perfect for him, but it just hadn't worked out that way. The bathroom stood empty for the first time at this time of day in the last week. This time yesterday and the day before and the day before would have marked the beginning of the evening routine, just minutes before they went to bed and went to sleep. Tonight was far from routine.

The hall remains silent for a further fifteen minutes or so. The two remain in their positions, tumbled on the floor, breathing in and breathing out, struggling to hold on.

The lights come first, and then the noise; the flashing blue and glowing red, the sirens, pulsing and spinning in unison. The light seeps in under the door, crawling into the flat through the windows and any crevice it can get under. It remains silent with just the lights for a few minutes more, the beige flat glowing red and blue, blue and red. Soon the police are surrounding the flat having received a report of a commotion and disturbance in the basement of Number 47. They can't hear anything now though. The street has returned to an eerie silence, no noise besides the odd street cat and a passing car. The tip had come anonymously from a neighbouring flat that clearly didn't want to get involved, but was concerned enough to call it in. They'd reported noise and violent sounding disturbances from the tiny, unassuming flat, and the growing silence in the street left the small number of police officers to approach with caution.

***

"Liam?" My voice floats in front of my face, disembodied and hollow. I can hear the croak and strain, the tin and the iron of my own blood coating my lips. I cough, blood spraying onto my hand. My eyes don't want to open. They hurt. Everything hurts.

I lift my eyelids just a slither. A strange flashing light is flooding the front half of my flat—the road facing side.

Red and blue. Blue and red.

I can't bring myself to open my eyes properly just yet. The lights are fine, pulsating to themselves. They're not disturbing anyone.

Red and blue. Blue and red.

My lungs fill about a third of the way with a painful breath. He's lying beside me, with his eyes fully closed. The light seems to be intensifying.

Red and blue.

The colours become more vivid and flash more intently.

Blue and red.

Oh God, I know what those lights are.

They must have worked all of this out. They must have realised that I've had Liam all this time—that he's been with me. He really has been missing because I took him and he's been living here, hidden in my basement flat. He didn't leave. He didn't run away like they'd said. He's been here all along.

Adrenaline gives me one final burst of energy. I struggle to my feet, tripping on the torn fabric of the silk red dress. I grab Liam under his arms and drag him to the bedroom, smearing his blood in a trail behind him, a crimson arrow pointing towards my door. A flashing neon sign. I drag his body up the short set of stairs, bumping his head over the ledges, over the carpeted hallway, and into the bedroom, shoving the door shut behind me. I don't know how the extra door makes me feel more secure, safer, but it does. Just a few more doors, a few more feet between me and the officers. A few more layers of protection. A few more layers to add to the lies. I lock the door and heave Liam onto the bed. He rests there, motionless, his arms twisted into gruesome, angular shapes. His face is contorted and snowy white. He looks awful. I did this to him. I don't know how, but I did. I'm surprised at my own strength, at my own perseverance. I drove his face into the door, I piled my body into him, and he hit back. He wanted to leave. He never wanted to love me. He'd always wanted to leave me, to blame me, to hold me responsible. And even after he retaliated, even though he attacked me back, I still love him. I look at him now, his face peaceful and calm, and after all that I still love him. After everything he's done, after trying to kill me, I don't care. I love him.

Liam

Over the thudding of my heart and the drumming in my ears, I still hear her. I can hear her breathing and whispering under her breath. *I love you. Don't worry Liam, I'll always love you.* She whispers it over and over, chanting a mantra, convincing herself. I can only just make out her words as my conscience drifts. My head is heavy and sinks into the floor. My limbs don't belong to this body anymore. They belong somewhere else. Somewhere where there is no pain, only floating. I'm numb from the concoction of emotions and wounds she's forced upon me. My eyes are sinking into my skull, further and further down into the warmth. Hot, sticky blood is coating one side of my face, crusting over and clinging to the tiny hairs on my skin. The pain is leaving me. My body is weightless, drifting over the macabre scene below.

Sarah

I roll off my tights and leave them on the floor. I slip the shiny, silk dress over my head, pleased at how soft it is as it brushes against my skin, draping over my cheeks. I'll fold it all later, when there's more time. I walk over to the other side of the bed, Liam's side, just to make a change in the routine. Change is good. I felt good in that dress. I felt attractive and powerful and feminine and commanding. I look down at my body now, just in my cheap nude underwear, smeared with someone else's blood. My body is covered in it. Patches of the red have darkened and congealed, scabbing on my knees and elbows where I slid across the carpeted hallway. I stand in front of the mirror for a while to come to terms with what's happened. I don't let it phase me. The blood is harsh and dramatic against my pale skin and bruising has started to flower across my face, spreading over my shoulders and dripping into the creases of my elbows. A faint, pulsing blue light reflects off the mirror and around my room. They're getting closer, and it's such a shame. A few more days' patience, and he may well have been mine. I know there's only one way out of this for me now—only one way that I can be with Liam forever. I close the mirror, my bloody fingerprints dotted over the surface, tiny stepping stones across the silvery glass. I catch a glance of him lying there, barely breathing. His head has fallen to the side at such an awkward angle, he can't possibly be comfortable. They'll never believe I had the strength to do that to him. He's just there, motionless, my captive, my prey, my trophy. I slide into the bed next to him, the cream bedding now grazed with my blood. I listen to his heart struggling to supply his body with what it needs. His chest rises weakly and falls raggedly with every breath. I brush away some of the blood from his face and neck. He's still beautiful, even now. Still captivating.

His low murmurs break the silence.

'Sarah, help,' he manages. His voice is barely a whisper, barely an enunciated breath into the room. 'Sarah, please.'

There's no answer. I can't speak. I know there's only one thing I can do to help him now. He'll die if I keep him here much longer.

'Sarah, please,' he rattles again. His voice is getting weaker, disappearing into the blue lights that have crept under my door. They'll be here any minute, but I don't let that phase me. They can't encroach on this, not until I let them. Not until I invite them to.

I turn on my side, shifting onto my elbow to face him. I kiss him, the iron taste of his blood filling my mouth, a mixture of his blood and mine, tangled together.

'I can't let you go, Liam. You tried to hurt me. You tried to kill me. And I love you, you know I do. I know that this isn't good for either of us now, but it's nearly over.'

I lay my head on his chest again, listening to his heartbeat. His breathing is thick and heavy with mucus and blood that's leaking into his lungs. The life is seeping out of his pores, the energy evaporating from his skin.

'I can't let you go. Not now I've finally got you.'

I breathe in his scent for a few more minutes as the lights grow brighter and the sirens grow louder. I quiet my breathing, sucking in tiny streams of air to stay as silent as I can. There's an abrupt knocking at the front door to the flat. It's strong and loud and steady. I don't know what to do when I hear it. Should I throw on a dressing gown, wash off the blood in a hurry and greet them at the door? Should I answer them as if nothing has happened? Would it be best for me to try to cover this up, make it last just a few more minutes before they give me no choice and take Liam away from me?

The knocking gets louder, more urgent. Quick raps against the wood, cold white knuckles bouncing off the shoddily painted door, causing the brass number to swing about and flail in the night air. I think they're shouting now, too. I can just about make out a few words, asking me to open the door. *Open up, or we're coming in, something along those lines.*

We'll give you to the count of something, but she can't quite make it out. Now she's drifting in and out of consciousness, her head sinking into his shoulder, her legs wrapped around his in a romantic embrace. Their shadowy silhouette is perfect. Tied together in passion, sleeping peacefully, embraced as two halves of one whole. It's only when the lights are turned on that you see the blood.

The knocking doesn't cease. Soon, they'll be forcing their way inside, and she knows it. Liam is stirring. He's drifting, just minutes away from his body giving up entirely. The colour has drained from his cheeks and limbs, leaving behind a grey husk. He knows he doesn't have long left. If she can't have him, then I suppose no one can.

She leans over him, her pale, unblemished skin brushing against his, ignoring his groans of pain and discomfort as she knocks a freshly seeping wound. Her hand cups his cheek, her eyes lock into his, and she kisses him one last time. She can tell it's nearly over. Her hand leaves his face and wanders over to the kitchen knife that still sits there, still rests on the bedside cabinet. It hasn't been used in days. She'd relaxed so much around him that she thought she may never need to threaten the use of it, let alone use it, again. Her fingers curl around it, blood staining her pearly fingernails a grubby red.

'It's okay, Liam. Shh, don't cry. Please don't cry.' She whispers to him in between her own tears, in between her sobs and the bubbles of phlegm clogging up her throat. 'Shh, please, Liam. They can't know we're in here. This is too perfect an ending for them to interrupt. Please, please be quiet,' she says, pressing the flat of the blade to his lips.

He trembles briefly at the cool touch of the steel. He shudders from the shock of the temperature, but not from fear, not anymore. He no longer has it in him to be afraid. She wipes the flat of the blade over his dry, cracking lips, into the dip of his neck and rests it against his ribs. He's not scared, but there are tears, maybe tears of relief or of desperation.

'Liam, please, you need to stop crying. I don't want to hurt you, but you need to be quiet. Do you understand?' She nods into the silent room as if he answered her loud and clear. She sits for a second, just breathing as quietly as she can and waiting, holding her breath to try to hear the commotion outside her front door. It'll be just seconds now, seconds until her perfect little world is shattered by a battering ram and police officers.

The commotion is getting louder. The thudding on the front door is definitely coming from something more powerful than a fist knocking in the cold air, searching for a lost gentleman. They know something's wrong and they're coming in to see what that is.

She leans back by his side, clutching the knife in her hand. She's whispering to him, singing softly under her breath.

'We'll be together again soon, Liam. You just need to stay quiet, as quiet as you can. I don't like a lot of noise. We need to stay so, so quiet. Just you and me. That's all we need. That's all we've ever needed.'

She listens to his fading heartbeat, each weak drum getting further and further apart from the last. Her face is coated with a thin sheen of tears and sweat. She listens to his raspy breaths, to the rattle in his ribcage. Just a few more seconds and this will all be over. She listens to the thudding at the door. To the thudding as it turns to slamming, to the slamming as it escalates to crashing. She listens to the door, her front door, being torn away from its hinges, splinters of wood and debris swinging lifelessly from the frame.

The yells are in her hallway now. The lights are stronger; they no longer have to creep under the doorframe to get in. It only takes seconds for them to start on the bedroom. They don't bother asking her to open up. The battering ram starts hammering into the door, the whole wall that supports it shaking under the force.

'This is where it all ends, Liam. I love you,' she says one final time, grabbing the blade and forcing the tip down into his stomach. The skin resists but quickly resigns and allows the knife to perforate the flesh. There's a gentle popping sound as the metal slides under, blood gushing from the wound and onto her hands. The door crashes from its hinges, falling in fractured pieces to the floor. Officers rush into the room and try to grab at the woman's arms. Unperturbed, she slides the knife deeper into his stomach, watching as he releases his final breath.